A QUICK STUDY

QUICKSILVER: BOOK TWO

JOSIE JAFFREY

CONTENT WARNINGS & SERIES RECAPS

There is a full list of content warnings at the back of this book, and also available at Josie's website at the link on the left below.

Recaps of the Silverse books are available on Josie's website at the link on the right below.

CONTENT WARNINGS

www.josiejaffrey.com/content-warnings

SERIES RECAPS

www.josiejaffrey.com/series-recaps

By Josie Jaffrey

Stories from the Silverse: the World of the Silver

The Seekers Series
Killian's Dead (short story prequel, free to Josie's subscribers)
May Day
Judgement Day
Winta's Day
Valentine's Day
Dark Days
End of Days

The QuickSilver Trilogy
Kill Me Quick
A Quick Study
Quick and the Dead
QuickSilver Omnibus Edition

The Solis Invicti Series
A Bargain in Silver
The Price of Silver
Bound in Silver
The Silver Bullet

The Sovereign Trilogy
The Gilded King
The Silver Queen
The Blood Prince

Silverse Serialised Stories
Dead Box
Dead Road

Silverse Short Stories
Encounters: Silverse Short Stories

Other Fiction

The Deluge Series
The Wolf and the Water

Short Stories
Broken Wings (collection)
Ring The Bell

1

IN THE MANSION on the Cooper River, Patience Quick was sleeping off a belly full of blood in the big four-poster bed of the grandest guest suite the house had to offer. It was occupied currently – and for the foreseeable future – by Kulika Yadav. The guest herself sat in an armchair by the bed and stared at the resting Silver she had just created.

She'd done the best she could for her. She'd bitten with all the gentleness she could offer, she'd caught Quick in her arms when the exhaustion of the turning and the covenant began to break her, then she'd stepped outside to find a human to drain into a glass so Quick wouldn't have to do any biting of her own.

Bartholomew decreed that all his crew drank from the vein, but...

Not yet.

Let her take it slowly, just this once. Let her not tear her way wildly into this new life the way Kulika had been forced to do, with hungry teeth and flesh beneath her fingernails.

Kulika watched the gentle thudding of Quick's pulse at her throat as she slept peacefully, counting every beat as a gift.

One thousand, eight hundred and fifty six. One thousand, eight hundred and fifty seven. One thousand, eight hundred and fifty eight.

Still her heart beat, thud after gentle thud, and Kulika's heart beat with it.

In the master suite next door, Bartholomew Sometimes-Roberts was flicking through the ledger of signatories to his Articles, counting each life as his due.

Two hundred and fifty six. Two hundred and fifty seven. And there on the final page – *two hundred and fifty eight* – the blood-inked signature that had finally brought Kulika back to him and sealed her place at his side forever.

Patience Quick.

With Quick bound to his covenant, and Kulika bound to Quick, she would never be able to leave him again, and that was everything his dark heart desired.

At least, it had been, until six months ago when *she* walked into his life and—

But he had vowed to himself that he would not remember that day, and didn't he have a solution to that particular problem right here at his fingertips? So instead he directed his mind back to the page, and forced a smile onto his lips. After a couple of seconds, it was not so very hard to keep it there.

Let Kulika have a few hours with the girl. Let her reflect on what she'd gained, and what she stood to lose at his merest whim. Let her have just enough time to realise how much was she was entirely in his power, then he'd demonstrate it in a way she would not forget.

His smile widened.

Over two hundred and fifty signatories, and Kulika besides. With that many Silver at his beck and call, he would have his war, and win it too.

* * *

On the Palisadoes – the narrow strip of land that connected Port Royal to the rest of Jamaica – Job Bayly crouched beside the road in an unremarkable spot and counted his buried treasures.

This stretch of sand had been a graveyard once, back before the earthquake of 1692 had sucked the old pirate capital under the sea. The island was sand all the way down, and that was what had doomed it. When the earth had shaken sand and water together, rocking and roiling on the join of two tectonic plates, it liquified the land until the whole peninsula was nothing but a gurgling morass of quicksand, swallowing everything in its path and spitting out only the bits it couldn't chew.

Bayly wouldn't have believed it himself if he hadn't seen it with his own eyes. When he looked out now along the dark expanse of the new quayside and closed his eyes, he could still remember exactly how it had looked more than three centuries ago. Port Royal hadn't just been a ramshackle collection of pirate huts and taverns along the shore, not like some of the old Caribbean settlements. Instead, its buildings had been raised ill-advisedly high on floor after floor of fine stone, with wharves and storehouses, churches and synagogues, and not just one but five stone-built forts to guard the harbour. The place had teemed with British soldiers and ships, both military and merchant vessels, and besides that the streets had been filled with buccaneers and privateers of every kind. It had been a bustling and licentious paradise, catering to every secret desire a pirate might harbour in their breast, or their belly, or below their belt. The locals used to brag that there was one tavern for every three residents, and the papers afterwards were full of stories about heavenly punishment, crowing that their god had seen fit to swallow Port Royal into the earth as a judgement on its wickedness.

Bayly thought that probably wasn't far from the truth. His own days in that port had been filled with drinking and debauching, but he'd been wickeder than most and yet here he was, still walking the earth in whatever kind of soulless form the clergy would condemn him and the rest of the Silver as inhabiting. Bayly didn't care much for their opinions either way. He'd never been one for moralising.

He liked the sunken city. He'd always been drawn here, enough that he came back often, and not just to check on his treasure, either. The place called to him like the ghost of a life half-lived, echoing through the centuries with memories of what might have been, pulling on him like an anchor tethering a ship to the sea floor. He dragged it along behind him in the sand, but it dug in deep, caught and held.

This graveyard called to him most of all. It had once been the final resting place of buccaneer supreme Henry Morgan. The gravestones were gone now, along with every other marker that might have led Bayly to the right spot, but he didn't need any guide beyond his own senses. He knew well enough where the 'X' was, no "digs" required.

He chuckled to himself at the private joke.

They were still down there, his secrets. He could sense them. Hear them, almost. They were fifteen feet under the sand, locked away in a lead box that had been dug up three times since it was first buried here, and only once by Bayly himself. That was the problem with treasure: everyone was always going hunting for it, like they had a right to what wasn't theirs. These treasures, though, Bayly would guard with his life – had guarded, in fact – and with good reason. One of them was enough to buy Enzo out of Bartholomew's covenant, if he reckoned it right, and that was a bargaining chip he wouldn't be surrendering to anyone.

Ever.

No matter who they were.

In the darkness, the sea looked like blood. Everything reminded Bayly of blood these days. The tide was gentle that night, each wave rolling in across the sand as softly as a breath, but when it withdrew it left the scrubby beach stained in ways that called unpleasantly on Bayly's more recent memories.

Not that he minded the bloodshed. He'd never flinched, not once. What he minded was the way the captain used that bloodshed to tarnish his crew, then polish them up afterwards into something that was shinier to his eye, more valuable.

Kulika saw the way of it clearly enough. Bayly had seen it just as clearly himself, but Bartholomew had tied him up in knots just the same, the way he did with everyone. There was no escaping it, no way except by blackmail and bribery, which was the way he'd got out the first time, or by overwhelming force, the way Kulika had.

It was her own damn fault that she was stuck there again. He'd warned her, more than once. She was the one who'd chosen to come back. Let her find her own escape hatch, because he wasn't giving up his. He had a neat solution to his own problems, and he was keeping it.

But oh, he did so hate it when things got messy.

Bayly laid a hand against the scrub-pitted, rocky sand and felt the pulsing call of the treasure beneath his fingertips. It would be time to dig soon. Soon, but not yet.

First, he had to do what he had been unable to accomplish in all these long months trapped in Bartholomew's net: convince Enzo that it was time to cut free.

2

IT WAS STILL dark when Quick was dragged unceremoniously from Kulika's bed and thrust out into the corridor beyond, where Monty was waiting for her. She got only a brief glimpse of Kulika's outraged expression and Bartholomew's dark smile before the door was slammed in her face.

She blinked the fog from her mind, trying to get her thoughts in order.

She'd been turned by Kulika, as evidenced by her overwhelmed senses.

She'd been marked by Bartholomew, as evidenced by the tattoo on her palm.

Then…

What?

She remembered the room spinning, and there'd been a glass of something she'd rather not think about at her lips – which she must have drunk mindlessly for all she could recollect it – and now here she was, bewildered in the corridor. There'd been no time to talk, or to ask any of the hundreds of questions she needed answered, right now.

What's going on in this mansion? What's going to happen

to us now? And, pressing on her with an urgency that Quick couldn't deny, *Does this mean that there is, in fact, an* us?

She wasn't going to get any answers from Monty, either, because the only thing he would say to her was, 'Back to the block,' before shoving her on ahead of him and falling into a sullen silence. When she started to talk, she just got another shove between the shoulders.

She could have run. She had the power now, didn't she? But then, where would she have gone? She couldn't just abandon Xiaoyu and the others in the blood cellar. Besides which, she needed to be here to find out what had happened to her best friend.

Kulika was looking for Evita too, she'd said. And whatever Xiaoyu said, Quick was sure she'd been trying to get her and the others out of the cellar. That meant Kulika was on their side, didn't it?

Then there was the covenant to consider. She'd signed the book, but she had no idea what any of it actually meant. It wasn't as though she'd been given the opportunity to read the terms and conditions, or to refuse them if she'd objected. None of it had been presented as though she had any choice in the matter.

It all came down to this: Quick had too little information and no plan at all. She obviously wasn't going to get anything out of Monty, so she decided she might as well do as he demanded and go back to the block. With any luck, she'd find someone there who was feeling more talkative.

But once Monty had directed her to the twenty-bunk dorm room she would apparently be sharing, initial signs weren't good.

'Here she comes,' a girl whispered quietly into the expectant hush.

Quick wasn't sure she would have been able to make out

the words twelve hours ago. Now that she was one of *them*, with her senses turned up to the maximum, every sound pinged around in her head like an angry scream of static. Her own footsteps sounded as harsh as a snare drum, even barefooted, and her heartbeat was so distractingly loud that she wasn't sure she'd ever be able to ignore it.

And the scents. Better that she didn't think too much about them, or she'd be dragged back into the memory of the fresh rush of Kulika's perfume through her sinuses when she took her first breath as one of the Silver, and forget herself all over again.

Kulika.

The few brief lucid moments they'd had together were torture to remember. Quick wanted so much of her, and she'd been allowed barely a taste. Now, with no idea when she'd see her again – if ever – she wondered if it might be better if last night had never happened at all.

'Who is she?' one of the girls asked, looking directly at Quick as she stood hesitating in the doorway where Monty had abandoned her.

'I'm Quick,' she spoke into the dim light. It probably should have been more than dim, perhaps entirely dark, but Quick could see better now, too.

'Not you,' the girl said again. '*Her*. The one who turned you.'

'Kulika?' Quick asked, and a sigh went around the room.

Kulika.

Quick knew she'd been hedging her bets when she'd chosen Kulika at the Casting, but she hadn't appreciated quite how much she'd overreached until that moment.

'I told you it was her,' a voice said from over by the window, then so many conversations started up that Quick lost track. She caught snippets: *pirate code... ran away and broke the covenant… definitely going to choose her.*

They recognised Kulika's name, that much was clear. What any of the rest of it meant was beyond Quick's comprehension, and she wasn't comfortable enough with her audience to start asking questions to clarify, or any questions at all. Instead, she made her way over to the first unclaimed bed she could find – a bottom bunk – and sat there, wondering what the hell she was supposed to do now. When they'd been climbing the stairs to this floor, Monty had said, 'Training starts later. Sleep now or don't sleep.' Those were the only words he'd spoken to her since leaving the mansion, so she should probably have taken them seriously, but the dorm was loud – *everything* was loud to her new senses – and she was haunted by memories that wouldn't leave her alone.

A kiss.

A bite.

A blissful moment of joyful release, like the surging chords of an anthem reverberating in her chest, then Bartholomew had stamped his covenant into her hand and the dream had ended.

This was the nightmare, now.

She stroked the black tattoo that sat in the centre of her palm. The skin had already healed, another ability her new being possessed, but the ink was trapped in there now.

She counted fourteen of them in the dorm room, including herself, and they all seemed to have the same mark. She recognised a few of the others from the Casting, but there'd been so many people in the hall that she couldn't be sure they were all new, like her. One of them she was sure about, though: by some miserable twist of fate, she'd ended up sharing a bunk with the girl who'd chosen Monty to turn her. Apparently, he'd been more successful with her than he would have been with Quick. She was hanging over the edge of the top bunk now, staring down at Quick with huge, brown, silver-threaded eyes. She had sharp cheekbones, tan skin, and long, straggly brown hair pulled into a messy ponytail that was draping straight down into Quick's face.

'Hi,' Quick said tentatively, brushing the girl's hair away. 'I'm Quick.'

'Oh, I know,' the girl said, 'Monty didn't stop bitching about you the whole way over here from the house.'

'Oh,' said Quick, because what was she supposed to say to that?

'Seriously,' the girl went on. '*I'm* the one who chose him. *I'm* the one who finally gave him a win. You'd think he'd be a little grateful or, I don't know, flattered at least, but oh no, he's all pissed off about you leaving him hanging instead.' She paused for a moment with a peevish look or her face, then added, 'I'm not, by the way.'

'Sorry?' Quick asked, having lost the thread entirely.

'Pissed off with you. I mean, obviously. I got what I wanted out of it. No complaints. About you, anyway.'

'Sorry?' Quick said again, still feeling like she wasn't really part of this conversation.

'I came here to turn Silver, and now I'm Silver, so even if Monty's going to obsess over you and ignore me like we didn't spend the past week fucking each other's brains out, then whatever, right? His loss.'

The girl's face disappeared and there was a *flump* from above, the bunk shaking as the girl settled onto the mattress. Apparently she was done talking, along with the rest of the dorm. They were quiet now, which gave Quick the distinct impression they'd been listening in to the conversation she'd just had.

It was an inauspicious start to Quick's time in the dorm,

but she had an ominous feeling that things were about to get much worse.

3

THE MORNING AFTER Kulika turned Quick Silver, the news broke. It started in Oklahoma, but it wasn't more than an hour before the rest of the country picked it up and ran with it. Now video of Cara Alton's Silver-speed abduction was playing nonstop on news channels, websites and social media worldwide.

The first clips hadn't given Kulika much cause for concern. The comments said it all.

I thought you were serious journalists, and now you're falling for crappy AI deepfakes? Give me a break.

Who's got their finger on the fast forward button?

Usain Bolt goes slower than this.

Nice try. Jog on.

But now, less than an hour later, speculation was surging out of control. Someone reputable had analysed the tape and declared it genuine. *Look,* one commentator said, *you can see vehicles moving in the background and they're going at normal speed, so how do you explain that if there's no doctoring?*

Then someone put Cara's parents in front of a camera. They'd already been badgering the local media to pay more attention to their daughter's abduction, which they'd always claimed was the result of a supernatural event. They'd been right there, they said. They'd seen it all. Or, rather, they *hadn't* seen it. One minute she'd been there and the next: nothing. Just her lemonade glass smashing on the paving and an empty space where she'd been standing just a millisecond before.

They were crazy, everyone had said. But now, four days later, with video evidence to back up their story, people were finally starting to take them seriously.

Bartholomew's opening volley had hit its mark.

Kulika was staring at the videos on her newly-returned phone when Bartholomew summoned her to the library. It wasn't a surprise. She'd been expecting the summons ever since he'd breezed through the connecting door between their rooms while it was still dark that morning and ushered Quick out with a brisk, 'Take her, kid.'

Kulika had protested, of course. She'd screamed and fought, for all the good it had done her. As Bartholomew had already demonstrated recently, he was more than capable of overpowering her.

'Settle down,' he'd said as he pinned her to the wall by her throat. As she'd thrashed hopelessly against his grip, her gaze had been drawn irresistibly to the copper coin he wore around his neck, the glinting token a shiny version of the tattoo that now scarred Quick's palm.

She'd stilled, then.

'You see how it is.' A gloating smile had tugged at Bartholomew's lips. 'You could have been my queen, Kulika,' he'd said, as though he were the one who'd been disadvantaged by her failure, and not Kulika. 'I would have been your slave,' he'd said. 'But instead...'

He'd let Kulika fill in the blanks.

'So fragile, these new Silver,' he'd said sadly. 'One little slip of the wrist, and—' Then he'd slammed his empty fist against the wall, punching a hole right next to Kulika's head. 'You understand the delicacy of the situation, don't you?'

Swallowing against his grip, Kulika had nodded awkwardly, her eyes fixed on his.

He'd released her, then. There would have been no point in holding her any longer; he'd already got her under control, broken and trained to his word.

'Stay here for the time being,' he'd said, as though it were an invitation rather than an order. 'I'll call for you in a while.'

The phone was a consolation prize, and a reminder: *everything you have is mine to give or take away.*

The photo of Evita Khalyed was missing from it now, along with every other bit of information Kulika used to have stored on it. He'd wiped it clean. She could still access the internet, though, so at least there was something to distract her while she waited for his next move.

If only the distraction hadn't been quite so cataclysmic in its implications.

Oklahoma Teen Snatched into Thin Air!

President Denies Military Tech Responsible for Teen's Disappearance

Supernatural Creatures in Our Midst?

The Silver were coming out, whether they wanted to or not. Maybe that wouldn't have bothered Kulika so much yesterday, but now that the Silver included Quick, she felt the threat of it jumping in her chest.

There was a knock at the door and a voice called, 'Bartholomew wants you in the library.' It sounded like the guy Bartholomew called "the kid", and everyone else called Monty. Kulika raced to the door, hoping to find out where he'd taken Quick, but the corridor was empty when she got there.

The coward had run away.

'Kulika,' Bartholomew greeted her as she walked into the library without knocking. 'How nice to see you, even if your arrival is a little… abrupt.'

'You were expecting me,' she argued in her defence, but even to her own ears the words sounded petulant.

Bartholomew's face softened into that look of paternalistic tolerance that she so hated, the one that said, *This child of mine is such a trial, but I am a caring and gentle parent, so I will weather it.* Kulika knew very well what Bartholomew really was, and she resented the gap between the persona he projected and the one he inhabited. She could see the width of that gulf, even if none of his followers would acknowledge it.

He was no father to her.

'Sit,' Bartholomew said.

Kulika made her way to one of the leather armchairs she'd occupied during their last discussion in this room, but Bartholomew stopped her before she could sit with an, 'Ah-ah-ah. I don't think so. Do you?' He raised an eyebrow at her, then held her gaze for a moment before looking regretfully at the bare floorboards.

This was how it would be, then. He'd welcomed her back into this house as a peer, and he'd offered her more than that besides. Now he wanted her to feel just how far she'd fallen, as though her loss of status were an unfortunate result of her own decisions instead of a punishment he was inflicting on her.

You could have had all this, he was saying, *if only you had appreciated what I offered you.*

Kulika reminded herself that he held Quick's life in his

hands.

She sat on the damn floor.

Bartholomew sat in the armchair and looked down at her like a master looking down at his dog, then he grinned his shit-eating grin.

Kulika wanted to punch it off his face, but instead she breathed deeply. She had borne this before. For Quick, she could bear it again.

'Can I see her?' Kulika asked.

'The crew are training until this evening,' Bartholomew replied dismissively. 'In the meantime, I've got a job for you.'

'You said no orders,' she reminded him, as ridiculous an assertion as that was while she was sitting on the floor at his feet. 'You said I could complete the mission I started for the baron.'

'Those were the terms of a different bargain though, weren't they?' he said condescendingly. 'As things stand, our deal has been completed, and we have no bargain at all between us now. But then we don't need one, do we?'

'No,' she agreed. They both knew she'd do exactly what he asked, whenever he asked, so what was the point in denying it? 'Would you let us leave?' she asked desperately, trying not to let her voice break over the words.

'Of course, *you* may leave,' he said magnanimously. 'You're not a member of my crew. You haven't signed the Articles. You're free to go whenever you wish.'

Kulika sat in silence, waiting for the rider she knew would inevitably follow.

'But why would you want to go when your heart is here?' he asked.

'Will you let *her* leave?'

'Why would she want to, when her crew is here? It's been

too long, Kulika,' he said, sitting back in his chair as though he were an old man reminiscing over fond memories, instead of a youthful immortal counting his victories. 'You've forgotten how strong the ties between a crew can be. Our *Patience* doesn't want to leave, does she?'

Kulika wanted to object to the *our*, but the truth was that, right now, Quick belonged more Bartholomew than she did to anyone, perhaps even more than Quick belonged to herself. That was what the covenant did, as Kulika knew from personal experience: it erased you and replaced you with the person Bartholomew wanted you to be.

'She refused to go with you last night, as I recall,' he added. 'When you wanted to leave?'

Even though Kulika knew he was twisting the event to his own purposes, she felt that barb land sharply in her chest.

'Only until she's found her friend,' Kulika argued weakly.

'Is that what she told you?' Bartholomew asked, with what sounded like pity. 'Did she say she'd be willing to go with you afterwards, or did you simply assume so? My dear girl, does she even know how you feel?'

'Yes,' Kulika insisted, but it sounded like the lie it was. They hadn't had the time to talk. There'd been the bite, and then she'd tried to get Quick to leave, and then Bartholomew had been there with his covenant stamp and she'd had to rush out to get blood for Quick to drink before she went feral and then...

Then it had been too late to tell her anything at all. 'If you'd just let me talk to her, then—'

'As it happens,' Bartholomew interrupted, 'I *am* willing to let you complete that little mission of yours.'

That had Kulika sitting up a little straighter, which irritated her; in her head she imagined herself as a pointer pricking up its ears.

But it was suspicious. Why, when his position was so strong, would Bartholomew grant her any concession at all? She was almost afraid to ask, for fear that the question would chase his generosity away, but she knew him better than that. If he was offering her even the tiniest crumb of consolation, there was a reason for it.

'Why?' she asked. 'Why do you care?'

'I care for all of my crew.'

'And Evita Khalyed was part of it? You didn't tell me that before.'

'Because you weren't crew before.'

'I'm not crew *now*. You just said so.'

Bartholomew just smiled at her.

As good as, she thought. She'd come back to this mansion swearing she wouldn't sign her life away again, and she hadn't. She'd let Quick do that for her, in ignorance of what her blood on the page would mean, and in ignorance of what would follow afterwards. She was still ignorant, in fact. She didn't know that Kulika had silvered for her. She didn't know that Kulika's life was now bonded to hers, or that Kulika was tied to Bartholomew just as surely as Quick was. More so, because he knew she'd do anything to protect Quick, even if it cost her everything in the world: her freedom, her pride, even her life.

Kulika was in love, and that love would be her undoing.

She couldn't say Bartholomew hadn't warned her. Back on the *Royal Fortune*, he'd always stressed that Article six was the most important one.

No boy or woman to be allowed amongst them. If any man shall be found seducing any of the latter sex and carrying her to sea in disguise he shall suffer death.

'Women, they're nothing but trouble,' he'd said to her. He'd said it loudly and often, not least every time they'd executed another crew member for breaking the code; more times than she could count. 'Let them under your skin and they'll sink you.'

And she'd nodded along, hanging on every word, believing to her bones that they were true.

No wonder he was crowing now.

'Tell me the rest,' she said now with a sigh.

'You asked me about Jane,' he said.

Kulika remembered. She'd heard the name from Quick, and—

'I told you she was one of the new Silver here at the mansion,' Bartholomew went on. 'And that's true, but the notable thing about Jane was that, unusually, she lost her memory when she was turned.'

'I've never heard of that happening before,' Kulika said, curious now.

'Me neither, but there it is. Apparently she had a sense of humour about it, though, because she called herself Jane Doe. She couldn't remember her real name, or where she'd come from, or how she'd come to turn Silver, but there were other things she could remember, like the geography and history and Charleston, especially as it related to the lives and deaths of the pirates who raided it.'

'That was Evita Khalyed's area of study,' Kulika said.

'Exactly.'

It was a subject Kulika had researched before she left Oxford. The whole reason Dr Khalyed had come to Charleston in the first place was to make a presentation to a bunch of academics and pirate fans about her research on the sinking of Port Royal. The 1692 disaster had happened before Kulika's time – she hadn't even been born to her human life back then – but she'd heard about it from Bayly and some of the others they'd sailed with. Apparently Dr

Khalyed had a theory based on relics recovered from the ruins of the sunken city. She theorised that some pirates were taking aliases throughout the buccaneering days of the late seventeenth century and the Golden Age of piracy that followed, reinventing themselves as new characters to evade capture. It was a pretty insightful theory, though she'd missed the essential detail that most of the pirates who did so were Silver, and they were reinventing themselves so no one would notice they weren't aging or dying like they should.

Now she'd lost her memory, she'd never know how right she'd been.

'So Jane and Evita Khalyed are the same person?' Kulika asked.

'It seems that way,' Bartholomew replied.

'And she was crew,' Kulika said.

'Yes.'

That made sense of so many mysteries that Kulika had puzzled over since arriving at the mansion. She'd known from Bartholomew's reaction to Jane's name that she was important to him. She'd also suspected from her snooping in his desk that he was keeping the missing person card with her picture on it somewhere close to him. And then there'd been that moment in the breakfast room when Quick had thrown herself at Kulika, saying, *I need to ask you about Jane*. She must have worked out that Evita had been going by that name while she was at the mansion.

So much made sense now.

'And she's already Silver?' Kulika asked.

'Yes,' Bartholomew replied.

'Since when?'

'She arrived here at the beginning of the year.'

'When exactly?' Kulika pressed, 'And how exactly?'

But Bartholomew just shrugged, as thought it were

irrelevant. Kulika didn't like that. It left too many questions unanswered. Maybe Bartholomew just hadn't paid attention, and he was certainly trying to give that impression, but it wasn't like him not to notice everything that happened on his property. It wasn't like him at all.

'The point is that she's gone,' he said. 'And you're going to find her.'

'Where did she go, then?' Kulika asked. 'Who saw her last?'

'Those are questions that no one seems capable of answering,' Bartholomew replied, with more than a little frustration. 'She was here, and then she was not.'

'When?'

'A few weeks ago.'

'That recently? Was she living in the house, or over at the block?'

'In the dorms,' he said. 'The others can show you her things. I don't know the details.'

He was becoming dismissive now, as though he wanted her to go away and do the task she'd been set instead of sitting here asking more questions, but he didn't tell her to go. Maybe he didn't want her to notice his discomfort, but she did. She noticed every glance away, every twitch of his fingers, every tiny slip of his smile. Those little observations were the only reason she'd survived as long as she had in this house the first time around.

She'd learned her master well, and she knew him well enough to know that if she threw him off his guard, she might provoke him into revealing more than he intended.

'Do you think she's dead?' she asked abruptly.

There it was: a slight widening of his eyes. It was evident for only the tiniest fraction of a second before he covered it, but Kulika saw it.

'She means something to you,' she said.

'I don't know what you're implying,' he replied calmly.

Kulika didn't know, either. She knew from the photo she'd seen that Dr Khalyed was a beautiful woman, but she also knew that her beauty would have had no effect on Bartholomew. In all his long centuries of celibacy, not a single person of any gender had raised any kind of romantic feeling in him. The question then became: what did she have that he wanted?

'Is it something to do with her research?' Kulika asked.

'Her work was of no consequence,' he said dismissively. 'I lived those years, along with the centuries before them, as well you know. I don't need some academic to tell me what pirates were like through the lens of three centuries of romanticisation. We *were* pirates, Kulika. Or have you forgotten?'

As if he would ever let her.

'Then why is she so important to you?'

'She's a missing piece,' Bartholomew replied with an innocent shrug. 'She's part of the crew, and when she left she took a piece of their power with her.'

Kulika raised her eyebrows at him.

'You might disbelieve it, but they can feel it,' Bartholomew insisted. 'They're part of each other, and they aren't complete when they're separated. Why do you think they all stay here? Her absence is like an ache in their blood. Either she needs to return to us or, if she's no longer alive, we need to recover her body.'

'So you can eat it?' Kulika asked, remembering the spectacle she'd witnessed earlier in the week.

Bartholomew gave her a disapproving look that made her reconsider her tone. She was pushing it, and the line he had drawn was not a flexible one.

'You disdain them without understanding their pain,' he said. 'Ask our Patience when you see her next, and she'll tell you. It eats at them. It drives them. You could let it drive you, too, if you would only surrender to it. You could join us, properly. It could be just like it was before,' he said, reaching down to caress Kulika's cheek. 'The two of us, together again.'

Kulika was confused, no longer understanding what place Bartholomew had ordained for her in his plan. Why, if he intended to elevate her, did he have her grovelling on the floor in front of him? He'd wanted to humiliate her, that was clear enough, but she'd assumed that humility was all he'd want from her now. He had Quick. He could give Kulika nothing but the dirt on his boots and he knew he'd have her at his command.

But he seemed to be offering her more than that: a place on the crew, as his first mate, at his side.

'Is that what you want?' Kulika asked.

'Of course,' he said softly. 'When I told you I wanted to give you rein to fulfil your darkest desires, that was more than just words. You have such unrealised potential, bottled and corked by Drake and the repressive mansion he runs back in the old country. Old indeed. Old-fashioned. Outdated, Kulika. All I've ever wanted is to set you free you from him, and now that you're home… I have so much to offer you, if only you would embrace your true self again.'

It would have been easier to dismiss his words as rhetoric if they hadn't struck her so deeply. Her sense of self had been on shaky ground ever since her return to Bartholomew's mansion, and now that she'd silvered for Quick – fallen in *love*, something she thought she'd never do – she could feel her identity splintering into pieces that were too fragmented to force back together again.

And the person Bartholomew remembered from their century together, that blood-soaked pirate who had cut down crew after crew in their never-ending quest for treasure? Kulika remembered her too, and with fondness, like a seductively comfortable cloak that she could step back into whenever she wanted, and find herself cradled in the anonymity of the dark. That was the persona into which Kulika had been birthed as one of the Silver. She was nostalgic for her in the way that most people are nostalgic for their youth: with envy for the power that rose-tinted memories attributed to her, but with equal scorn for her mistakes, believing rashly that she could not make them again.

Kulika understood well enough why that memory was so seductive to her. She understood less why it preoccupied Bartholomew.

'Why offer me anything at all?' she asked.

'I made you Silver,' he said, cupping her face in both of his hands, then he leaned down to press his forehead against hers. Kulika couldn't look away, and not just because he was holding her in place. His gaze was like a cage, trapping her attention. Her eyes watered as she stared into his. 'You are mine,' he whispered, 'and I am yours.'

'And Quick?' she whispered back shakily.

'Is crew,' Bartholomew replied, 'and the crew is ours. Yours and mine.'

'Ours,' she repeated.

'Always.'

Then Kulika blinked, and the moment broke. Bartholomew released her face and relaxed back in his chair as though it had never happened, smoothing the sleeves of his henley.

'So, you see,' he said briskly, 'you won't be finding Evita

Khalyed for Drake's sake at all. You'll be doing it for the crew.'

For the crew.

The words were painfully familiar.

'All right,' Kulika said heavily. 'For the crew.'

'That's my girl.' Bartholomew smiled, and three hundred years melted away.

That's my girl, he'd said as she blinked back to consciousness after slaughtering half the hands on board their prize during the thirst of her turning.

That's my girl, he'd said as she savaged her way through blades and gunfire to get to his body and hurl it overboard, as they'd agreed, on the day the pirate Bartholomew Roberts had apparently died taking grapeshot in the neck during sea battle with the *Swallow.*

That's my girl, he'd said as she finally sank her hand into his chest and brought it out holding his heart, on the night she'd left the mansion behind her for what she'd vowed would be the last time.

For the crew, she'd spat back at his unconscious body, but what she'd meant was, *for myself.*

Now, Kulika had no crew any longer, nor any self that was worth saving. There was just Quick, and *her* crew, and the captain they all served.

4

'EVERYONE UP!' CAME a shout from the corridor, accompanied by what sounded like someone hitting a saucepan with a spoon. 'Out of bed, you lazy fucks!' the shouting continued along the corridor. 'Training starts and ends today, so get your butts downstairs!'

'Language!' someone shouted back.

'Oh, fuck off, you puritanical shit.'

'Lord, listen to the mouth on you.'

'And look at the ass on you. You don't hear me complaining.'

'He don't get no complaints about that ass!' a third voice joined in, then the block echoed with brittle laughter bouncing off the empty walls.

It wasn't the way Quick would have chosen to wake up, but right now she didn't want to wake up at all. Given the alternative, she supposed, she should be grateful. So many of the people who had walked into the hall last night weren't alive to see this morning.

Quick had overheard the women in the bunk next to hers talking about it during the night.

'I heard fifteen percent,' one had whispered. 'That's what

Josh said, anyway.'

'Your sire?'

'Right. Good numbers, he said.'

'Eighty-five percent of us dying is *good*?'

'According to him. Guess we should count ourselves lucky.'

'Luckier than most, sounds like.'

A few more people had joined the dorm overnight. Some of them cried. That was a surprise. Quick had thought she was the only person who didn't want to be part of the Casting ceremony last night, so she wasn't expecting anyone else to be sad about turning vamp. Maybe they'd lost people they'd come here with, she thought, or maybe she'd just been dead wrong to think she was alone in her unwillingness. Either way, she couldn't see any red eyes once the curtains were flung open to let in the dawn sunlight, so she couldn't pinpoint her possible allies. Right now, surrounded only by eyes threaded with silver, she couldn't trust anyone at all.

Quick had slept in her clothes, covered only by the robe she'd worn to the ceremony last night. She wasn't sure what this training would entail, but a loose cotton dress didn't seem like ideal attire. Looking around the room at bikini tops and suits and ball gowns, none of them with any shoes at all, it seemed like Quick wasn't alone in being unsuitably dressed. They weren't given an opportunity to change. Instead, the long-haired, anchor-bearded man that Quick knew as Brandon came to the door and yelled, 'Downstairs, now!'

Her bunkmate jumped down from above and walked out without giving Quick a second glance. The others followed her, whispering as they went, filing out of the room in pairs and threes. It all gave Quick the feeling that she was the odd one out. She merged into the pack quietly, watching, listening. The others were mostly younger than Quick, and they all seemed to know each other. Beside them she felt grey and dirty, because compared to them, she was. None of them had come here from the blood cellar, she was sure now, and that showed not just in their appearance, but in their attitudes too. They weren't terrified captives, too scarred by loss to allow themselves to make new friends, or even idle conversation. They'd come here from the poolside, or from the house, or from parties where they'd gone with styled hair and tight clothes, expecting a good time. Their hair was messier now, their make up a little smeared by pillows and sheets, but they tidied each other up on the way down the stairs so that by the time they'd all traipsed through the common area on the ground floor and out into an open space behind the building that Quick had never seen before, they looked ready to go out all over again.

'Line up against the wall!' Brandon yelled, pacing away from the building so he could get a good look at them all.

Quick inserted herself somewhere in the middle of the crowd as more people poured out of doors in other parts of the building, doors she hadn't even realised were there. The whole structure was C-shaped, with two wings about half the length of the main section projecting off the back to cup around this wide area of open dirt.

All in all, there were about sixty of them lined up against the bare breeze-block walls when they'd all finally congregated, enough that they couldn't all have been turned Silver the previous night. There had only been a couple of hundred people in the hall, and at a success rate of fifteen percent, the maths wasn't hard: there were double the number there should have been. As was evident from the more comfortable clothes that some of those who'd arrived later were wearing, part of their number had been expecting this.

'Training time!' Brandon yelled, settling a pair of plastic sunglasses onto his nose. He was wearing bright, multi-coloured Bermuda shorts slung low on his hips and a lilac tank top that bared his tanned arms to the early morning sunshine.

In the shade of the building, it was cold enough to make Quick shiver, but Brandon's next words made it clear that she wouldn't be shivering for long.

'Running, jumping, fighting,' he said. 'Now that you've all turned, you can move super fast, jump super high, and hit really fucking hard. You've got the day to mess around out here teaching yourself how to do all that, then you're out of time. Some of you who were turned earlier have had a week or two to practice already,' he added, which explained the extra numbers, 'so you can show the others how it works.'

'Most of you are going to suck,' said Bella from the sidelines. She was leaning in the doorway of one of the wings, dressed in a patterned satin robe with pyjamas underneath. She had her hands wrapped around a steaming cup of what Quick would have bet anything was coffee. Quick watched enviously as Bella sipped it.

'Nice of you to get out of bed and join us,' Brandon said to Bella. 'You going to help?'

'Nope, just here to heckle,' she said.

Brandon looked like he was going to argue, but then a handful of other vamps came out of the door behind her, with Monty in the lead.

'I'll take it from here,' he said to Brandon, who raised his hands and stepped aside. The dynamics were strange. Either there'd been some kind of hierarchical rearrangement amongst the vamps, or turning that girl Silver had done more for Monty's status than Quick realised, because for now he seemed to be absolutely in charge.

'Angelina,' he said, holding out his hand towards them.

Along the line a few yards to Quick's right, the girl who had the bunk above hers – the girl Monty had turned – stepped forward with a smile and jogged over to take his hand.

'Show them what you can do,' he said to her.

Angelina smiled again, smugly this time, then she moved. And Christ, did she move. One moment she was standing calmly at Monty's side, and the next there was a whirlwind-raising blur along the line of spectators before she reappeared on his other side, having circled the entire training ground in a fraction of a second. Quick was barely recovering from that disorienting sight when Angelina moved again, this time jumping in a single massive leap from the ground until she stood on the far corner of one of the wings of the building, looking down at them from several storeys above Quick's head.

'That's what you're aiming for,' Monty said.

Angelina landed gracefully on the ground and sauntered over to join him once more, then he turned to her, dropped a kiss on her cheek and whispered something that not even Quick's new senses could pick up. She heard Angelina's answering giggle, though, so she could take a pretty good guess.

'Once you've mastered that,' Monty said, 'you can start sparring. Get to work.' He didn't need to shout, as Brandon had. By the end of Angelina's demonstration, it was quiet enough that when everyone started muttering, the whispers crashed over Quick like waves.

Some kind of prodigy.

Why her?

Thought it took months to learn.

All the while, Angelina stood in the sun and beamed.

Quick didn't rush to compete with her. Instead, she stood by the wall for a while and watched as the others ran around the perimeter of the packed-dirt space. A few grasped the skill immediately and moved on to jumping, with less success, but most of them were still running around aimlessly at normal speed when Quick decided she couldn't put it off any longer.

She had things to do, namely finding Evita and rescuing the people in the cellar, somehow. If she was going to have any hope of doing those things, then she'd need all the powers she could muster, and soon.

She took a deep breath and pushed away from the wall.

The moment Quick stepped out from the shadow of the building, her skin began to burn. It wasn't just turning pink, either; it was puckering and spitting, like it was sizzling against direct flame. For a second, she just stared at it, unable to process what was happening, then someone slammed into her in a waist-high tackle, shoving her back into the shade. Her head cracked back against the wall, leaving her ears ringing and blood in her mouth. She must have bitten her tongue, she guessed.

Then the screaming pain of the burns rushed in, boiling along her bare arms, up her neck, across her face. There was a shrieking noise that sounded like a dying animal, which she soon realised was coming from her. *She* was the animal, and it certainly she felt like she was dying. She tried to look down at her arms, imagining she'd see only a blackened and charred mess of bones and immolated muscle, but she couldn't open her eyes. Her eyes were sealed shut. Her eyes had been *burned* shut.

She shrieked again. She could hear Monty talking, yelling

at her, but she couldn't make out the words between her own screams. Her skin was peeling off her body in sticky wet strips and she was going to die like this, in the worst way she could imagine, melting into a puddle of pain and ash in the dirt.

Then a quiet voice said, 'I'm here,' and her body stilled of its own accord.

She was still in pain – incredible amounts of pain that blazed along every part of her exposed skin, then tightened at the places where her dress rubbed against it – but it was as though the pain had been moved into a different box, off to one side. She knew it was still there, and she could feel every bit of it, but it wasn't occupying her mind the way it had moments before. Instead of imagining her arms burning away in front of her sightless eyes, she became a breeze riding over the ocean, breaking across the bow of a wooden-hulled ship to chase up into the rigging and pull strands of blonde hair across welcoming sea-grey eyes.

'I need to touch your skin,' the voice said.

Quick should have protested, because her skin was *on fire*, but as her mind's eye skipped through the salty air, she was distracted by the gentle cresting of cold dawn light over the horizon, and she surrendered to it.

She felt a hand slip around the back of her neck, sliding beneath her hair to cradle her head, then her mouth filled with fresh water. She swallowed, and a relieving cold pooled at the back of her neck at the point of the hand's contact, then broke over her, cooling her skin, rolling her into its undertow in an embrace that gathered in her chest and burst out through her body in rush of sea spray.

When she sat up and opened her eyes, she did so with a gasp, like a diver coming up for air.

'Are you okay?' Monty asked. He was crouching beside

her on the ground, his face a mask of concern, but no one else in the crowd gathered around them was looking at him. They were looking at the woman on Quick's other side, the one who was staring intently at a canteen as she screwed the top back on.

Kulika.

'Better?' she asked, her gaze still fixed on her task.

'Better,' Quick replied with disbelief.

And she was. She looked down at her arms and saw only clean, unscarred skin. She touched her face and eyelids to find them smooth and painless under her fingertips. If it wasn't for the layer of ash that now surrounded the spot where she was sitting, she might have thought she'd imagined the whole thing.

'Good,' Kulika said. 'Pale skin? You get sunburnt easily?'

'Yes…'

'It happens this way sometimes. You'll be sensitive for a while, until your body adjusts,' Kulika said softly, then she stood and turned to Monty. 'Cover her up and get her some sunblock. Do not let her burn again.' The threat in her tone was understated, but it was there.

Then Kulika was gone. She just disappeared, leaving a susurrus of whispered gossip in her wake as the crowd dissected Kulika's brief cameo.

'What happened?' someone whispered.

'Must have been blood in that bottle,' someone whispered back. 'Healed the new girl up. Kind of reassuring, right?'

'Makes me want to carry a bottle of the stuff around.'

'Captain says we only drink from the vein.'

'But *she* doesn't have to? What gives?'

'That was Kulika Yadav,' a third voice chipped in. 'Keep your voice down.'

'Shit,' the first voice whispered, and it sounded fearful.

Whatever status Kulika had to these people, it didn't fill Quick with confidence. In fact, it sounded like it should make Quick wary.

But hadn't Kulika come to Quick's rescue? Hadn't she saved her from the fire? It was more than any of the others had done.

Yet all the while, she hadn't even looked at Quick.

Not once.

'Shit,' Monty breathed. 'Do you need more blood? Are you hurt, or—'

'I'm fine,' Quick said, a little confused.

The whisperers had mentioned blood, too, but Quick was sure it had just been water she'd drunk. Hadn't it? She struggled to untangle the threads of what had just happened, because there had been a distinct hallucinatory quality to it all. One minute she'd been burning, then there'd been the breeze and the sea and the water in her mouth...

But she must have been mistaken. In the trauma of the moment – she had nearly *burned to death*, after all – perhaps it wasn't surprising that her mind had taken her away somewhere else, somewhere that transformed fire into a breeze and blood into water. It must have been blood she'd drunk or she wouldn't have healed. That was just how vampires worked.

'You could have warned me about the sunburn,' Monty said to Quick.

'I think you mean that *you* could have warned *me*,' Quick replied, snapping at him because she was too jittery to control her tone. 'What else is suddenly going to be life-threatening now? Should I be avoiding garlic and crosses, too?'

'Very funny,' he sneered, before getting to his feet and ambling off into the block.

Quick hadn't been joking. She was shaking from the adrenaline rush and crash of the last ten minutes, so instead of going back to training with the others, she just sat against the wall and tried to calm herself down while she waited for Monty to come back with some suncream. She assumed that's where he'd gone, anyway. She hoped it was, because the sun was getting higher all the time, and she wouldn't be in the shade much longer.

None of the others tried to talk to her, about Kulika or the burning or anything at all. In that respect, at least, it looked like she would be remaining in the dark.

5

'KULIKA,' BARTHOLOMEW CALLED out of the porch door.

Kulika hadn't asked his leave to go and help Quick before running out of the library, but really, what had he expected her to do? She'd felt Quick's pain rip through the bond, burning through the cord that tethered Kulika to her until it threatened to snap entirely. Bartholomew had said it himself: the new Silver were fragile. An injury like that, to so much of her body, with flames that were still burning when Kulika had—

She didn't want to think about it. She didn't want to remember the image of Quick lying on the ground like that with fire dancing up her limbs, black smoke rising and blood spitting, but she knew she'd be seeing it in her nightmares from now until the day she died.

Which could so easily have been today. If Kulika had reached Quick a few seconds later, they would both have burned up in that fire.

'Kulika,' Bartholomew called again and, like a faithful mutt, she came to heel.

'I had to,' she said, running up the porch steps. 'She

would have died.'

Bartholomew didn't reply, he just gave her a disappointed look and turned away, walking back into the house.

Bayly was leaning against the porch rail drinking his coffee, as he usually did at this time of the morning, and probably wishing he was anywhere else. Kulika caught his sympathetic eye for a moment before she hurried inside after Bartholomew.

'You know I had to,' she insisted. 'You *know*.'

He didn't turn around, he just kept walking until they were back in the library, with Kulika trailing at his heels the whole way. He shut the door behind them.

When he moved towards Kulika, at first she thought he was going for her neck again, so she flinched and backed up until her shoulder blades hit the door. Instead, he reached out to touch her face, trailing his fingers across her cheek as though they belonged there, then pressing his thumb gently to her forehead as though in benediction. It was a gesture she'd received a hundred times or more, on the ship, before.

'We have some trust still to rebuild between us. Don't we?' he said.

Bartholomew had been a priest once. He'd known how to make his congregants feel like the eye of god was watching over them, in the same way that he knew how to make his crew feel like their captain's eye was watching now, and not always benevolently. He blessed and cursed with equal iniquity, and all they could do was count the blessings when they got them. Kulika knew she should take this one and run.

'I'll do whatever you want,' she said desperately. 'You know that. You can trust my feelings for her.'

'But I need to trust your feelings for *me*,' he said mournfully. 'I need you to believe in what I'm trying to build here.'

'Which is?'

He turned to the side for a moment, clenching his jaw, as though he was trying to find the right words, as though he hadn't had every one written and rehearsed in advance. Kulika thought it was an act at first, but when he spoke again, he did so with such emotion that she found herself doubting her own assumptions.

'I know you hate this place,' he said, gesturing around at the book-lined shelves of the library. 'This hemmed-in building, and the walls of words I have to write to keep us all together here as a crew. My god, we were *pirates*. There was nothing *but* the crew, and the plunder, and the open waves. I know you resent being beached in this mansion, and that you always did, but do you really imagine that I don't resent it too?'

In truth, Kulika had never considered it. Bartholomew was the *captain*. He was in command. He told them what to do, and when to do it, and although he'd always told them he was acting for the good of the crew, only an idiot would have failed to see the glint of megalomania in his eyes. She'd just assumed that he was following his own whims, doing whatever he wanted and dragging them along for the ride, because it had always appeared that way. He'd never given the impression that he wasn't completely happy in his lordship of this mansion, but then coming here hadn't exactly been a choice either. The Golden Age of piracy had ended, the great protagonists of the time had either been hanged or forced into hiding, and the crew of the *Royal Fortune* had little choice but to do the same.

'We did what we had to do, to survive,' Kulika said, echoing the words that Bartholomew had spoken to her so many times during those first days on land in the Carolinas.

'I want to do more than just survive,' Bartholomew said.

'Yes, the world changed, but now we finally have the power to change it back again. Don't you see?' He took her hands in his, clasping them as though they were a lifeline in a storm. 'Haven't we waited long enough to become again the people we have always been? *Pirates*, Kulika. *Vampires*. We don't settle, we roam. We don't ask, we take. We don't hide, we *ambush*. It's time that you remembered who you are. Who we all are. I only want to remind you.'

'I remember, Bartholomew.' She remembered so vividly that it scared her. Those memories should have turned her stomach – once, at the end, when she'd left here with Baron Drake, they had done exactly that – but now they gave her a thrill that uncomfortably straddled the space between horror and desire.

And was that really such a bad thing? She was bound to Quick, and so bound to Bartholomew. If he was going to use her as his instrument of destruction either way, then perhaps it wasn't so terrible an idea to harden herself to his violence, just a little. Not enough that she would cross the line into savagery, just enough to shield herself so that she didn't end up breaking herself in her efforts to shield Quick. She could allow herself that much free rein.

'I want to give you that again,' he said, looking into her eyes. 'A life where we don't have to compromise on who we are, where we're not fettered by having to hide our needs and desires. A life of freedom; for you, and me, and for our Patience, too. Isn't that something you want as much as I do?'

'I…'

'I remember that night on the beach in Hispaniola,' he whispered seductively as he squeezed her hands in his. 'Washing off the blood in the shallows, piling the fire high on the sand, then drinking our fill and more from the prisoners we took from that prize off the Windward Isles. And then, when the embers smouldered down...' His eyes locked with Kulika's, and they burned.

She burned too.

She'd forgotten that night. Repressed it, even.

Heat shivered across Kulika's skin, bringing incongruous images of Quick flooding into her mind, muddling them with the memories of Hispaniola. Her recollections of Quick's accident that morning should have been unpleasant – the fire, the burning – but instead Kulika remembered the moment she'd healed Quick with her touch. She felt again Quick's smooth skin pressed against the palm of her hand, and the teasing softness of Quick's hair as Kulika slid her fingers into it, connected to their bond, and unleashed herself in a wash of healing energy. There had been catharsis in that moment, the same kind of catharsis she'd felt that dark night on the beach in Hispaniola as she'd taken that willing woman in her arms, as they'd pulled each other out of their clothes and, finally, for the first time, Kulika had slid her fingers into—

She'd known Bartholomew had been watching, somewhere out in the darkness of the dunes.

Back then, Kulika hadn't objected; he'd always had his eyes on her, and she'd found comfort in his omniscience. She'd known later – much later – that she should have objected, because it wasn't right, was it? But so much of what they'd done in those days was wrong, and no one had been keeping score. They were *supposed* to do wrong. Like Bartholomew said, they were *pirates*. They roamed, they took, they ambushed. They *lived*, and they made no apologies for it. Bartholomew had certainly never made any, and Kulika hadn't felt he owed her them.

She'd known he was watching that night, and she'd

undressed her prize on the beach anyway. Maybe that was even why she'd done it, because – god help her – she'd *liked* it.

'Every night could be Hispaniola,' he whispered, and her skin burned where his breath touched her cheek.

When Kulika saw that night in her mind again now, the person in her arms wasn't the anonymous woman who'd taken her virginity, every detail about her forgotten in the haze of blood and rum and time. Instead, it was a woman with lips that tasted like autumn berries, skin that smelled of freshly-cut flowers, and sunset-red hair that glinted in the firelight as it spread across the sand.

As Kulika lay back against the door to the library with past and present flickering together in her mind, she knew Bartholomew was watching, tracing her reactions by the flush of her cheeks, the scent of her arousal and the sticky touch of her palms as she lost herself somewhere between fantasy and memory. Still, she didn't want him to stop. The truth was, she'd missed having his eyes on her.

'All I want is to see you take what you desire,' he whispered, and some part of her that she'd been denying for a hundred years stretched and twisted in her core.

There was a knock at the door behind Kulika's head.

'What?' Bartholomew barked angrily, his gaze still locked with hers.

'Um,' a voice mumbled from the other side. 'You wanted me to bring Jane's stuff?'

Finally, Bartholomew released Kulika's hands and broke eye contact so he could guide her gently away from the door and wrench it open. She was still trying to get a hold of herself when he dismissed Monty and turned back to her with a small cardboard box in his hands.

'Go on,' he said, his annoyance at the interruption spilling over as he tipped the box out onto the table. 'Look through her effects. Talk to the newer crew. Find out what you can.'

His rapid change in mood made Kulika want to reclaim the charged atmosphere of a few moments before, however uncomfortable it made her. The switch had been so abrupt it shocked her, but it didn't surprise her. Bartholomew had always been a mercurial creature.

'In here?' she asked.

'You can use this room. I've got business elsewhere,' he said dismissively, as though he hadn't just given her free rein of his inner sanctum. It was a mark of trust, however casual he made it seem.

He gives and he takes, Kulika reminded herself, but it was hard not to feel the approval in the gesture, as he no doubt intended that she should do.

It was enough to make her hope, recklessly.

'And afterwards?' she hazarded.

Kulika waited for a moment, praying that he'd reward her with something more, so she wouldn't have to ask for it herself. He was not so magnanimous, though. He liked to feel the power he had over people. He wanted them beg.

'Surely you're not asking to see our Patience again, so soon?' he said, with what sounded for all the world like real concern. Then he chuckled. 'Have patience, and you will have *Patience.*'

It was a hollow joke. Kulika didn't laugh.

Bartholomew sighed, disappointed with her again.

'Search the girl's things,' he said irritably. 'When you're done, the kid can get the crew to come and speak to you in turn, and perhaps you'll be able to learn something he couldn't. I'll be back this evening, and then we'll talk.'

'And if I find something?' she said. 'Where will you be?'

'Away,' he said, then he left her alone in the library,

slamming the door behind him.

6

QUICK COULDN'T DO it. She'd run and jumped in the meagre shade of the building all day, until her feet had bled and healed fifty times over, but she still couldn't get faster than a normal sprint or higher than a normal jump. She hadn't even tried sparring; everyone else had paired up without her. Maybe that was for the best. Given the way things were going with the running and jumping, she would only have ended up pummelled to pieces anyway.

The others had all given up and gone inside by now, half of them having successfully mastered at least one of their powers, but Quick was going nowhere. Now that the sun had dipped beneath the horizon, she could finally stop worrying about staying in the shade and concentrate properly on what she was trying – and failing – to do.

The door to one of the common areas opened behind her and a familiar voice called out, 'Hey, you thirsty yet?'

Quick turned, panting, to see Penny standing in the doorway dressed in sweatpants and a strappy T-shirt. She hadn't forgotten that Penny was one of the vampires who'd helped Monty throw her down into the blood cellar that first night, so no wonder Penny's demeanour was tentative now.

She hovered by the door, her expression somewhere between hope and concern.

'I'm fine,' Quick said, turning back to her drills.

'The others are refuelling,' Penny said. 'You know. With blood.'

That got Quick's attention. 'From the blood cellar?' she asked.

'They're in the big common room. They're nearly done, so we'll be putting the humans back down through the hatch soon, but I saw you hadn't come in yet and… Thing is, if you don't drink the blood, you're never going to make this work. You need it to power the Silver speed and all the rest, and you're not always going to get the chance to fuel up, so I'm just saying.'

'Saying what?'

'Take it.' Penny pushed the door open wider, holding it open for Quick.

Quick didn't trust her. She couldn't, not after Penny had so happily participated in her incarceration, but no one else in this place seemed willing to speak to her at the moment. At least if she went with her, she might get some answers.

'After you,' Quick said as she reached the door, not wanting to let Penny get behind her. She got a hurt look in return, but Penny did as Quick asked anyway.

'It happened to me too,' Penny said as they picked their way through the furniture, empty beer bottles and snack detritus carpeting the small common room on the other side of the door. 'I'm not saying that makes it any better, but I didn't ask for this either. I was in the blood cellar too, in the beginning.'

'I think that actually makes it worse,' Quick said quietly.

'And I'm not…' Penny trailed off as they reached the corridor, then turned back to face Quick. 'I'm not going to apologise, because I didn't have a choice in what I did, any more than you do now.'

Quick laughed at how ridiculous that sounded. 'You're a vampire. I was human. You put me in your *blood cellar* so you could drink my *blood*.'

'I drink the blood because without it, I'll die. You'll die without it, too. I put you down in the cellar because that's what I was ordered to do, for the crew, and because we have to get our blood from somewhere.'

'Just following orders?' Quick asked sarcastically.

'Don't be facetious,' Penny hissed. 'You are *one day old* in this place. You have no idea what it's like here. What it's been like, for months.'

'Then tell me.'

'I'm not sure I can even put it into words,' Penny said, looking hopelessly into Quick's eyes. 'We're all prisoners here, one way or another. It's not just that if any of us left, the others would track us down and drag us back, dead or alive. There's something else, too. I don't know if it's something in the blood, or something about *him*—'

'Him?'

'Bartholomew,' Penny said in a voice that was little more than a whisper. 'He never comes over to this block, but then he doesn't have to, because you can almost feel him watching anyway. And Kulika...'

'What about her?'

'Well...' Penny raised her eyebrows at Quick.

'What?'

'You've got to be wondering why none of the others are talking to you.'

'They're cliquey bastards.'

'*You're* the cliquey bastard. You got turned by Kulika Yadav. Don't you even understand what that means?'

'Last call!' came a shout from along the corridor.

'You'd better go,' said Penny. 'Third door on the left.'

'What does it mean?' Quick asked.

'Later. Go on.'

'Last call! Going in ten, nine, eight, seven…'

'You're not coming?' Quick asked.

'I can't be seen talking to you,' said Penny, horrified. 'Now go.'

'…three, two…'

Penny pushed Quick off along the corridor, then disappeared in the opposite direction, leaving Quick to walk through the door just as the countdown reached zero.

Brandon had been the one doing the counting.

'Here she is,' he said, flicking his hair over his shoulder as she walked in. 'Always making an entrance.'

'Making a scene, more like,' said Angelina.

Juvenile, Quick thought. The block might feel like a college dorm, but she didn't have to act that way. Didn't they have enough to worry about?

'Hello, Angelina,' Quick said cordially as she walked into the room, determined to be friendly. Then she took a proper look around and froze on the spot, just a few steps from the door.

The "big" common room was certainly that. It had floor-to-ceiling windows along one wall, and was filled with groups of Silver gathered on sofas and beanbags, drinking and chatting and laughing. There was one enormous television on the wall on this side of the room, showing a first-person shooter game that the nearest group of Silver were whooping at, and another at the far end, displaying some kind of list on the screen. The party mood became uncomfortable the moment Quick noticed a handful of bedraggled humans arrayed against the side wall to her left, bleeding from the neck.

Xiaoyu was amongst them.

'Shit,' she said to Quick. 'It worked, then?'

'It worked,' Quick replied quietly.

'Okay, back downstairs,' Brandon said to the humans, then he added to Quick, 'You drinking?'

'I don't...' Quick looked around the room, noting all the people looking on with barely veiled interest, then looked back to Xiaoyu and the line of humans. What did they expect her to do? Just pounce on someone and bite them while the others played video games in the background, like that was a perfectly normal and not at all surreal thing to do?

'Performance anxiety?' Angelina teased her.

Brandon gave Angelina a long-suffering look, then turned to Quick and said, 'You can drink in there.' He pointed to an open door, close to the other end of the space, which led to a small room with another television. 'You, snarky girl,' he said to Angelina. 'Help me get the others back downstairs. You two as well,' he added, beckoning over a couple of spectators from a nearby sofa.

They groaned.

'Get used to it!' Brandon yelled at them. 'Fresh meat does the chores. Now get off your asses so I can go sit on mine.'

It was only when they started leading the humans out of the room that Quick realised they were leaving her with Xiaoyu.

'Wait, I can't—'

Xiaoyu sighed. 'You can,' she said, then she turned and led the way to the little room Brandon had indicated.

Quick looked at the faces of the other Silver, watching her blithely and with only half an eye as they lounged around on sofas and beanbags, drinking and playing games and relaxing. It felt incongruous. They'd just been biting people in here and drinking their blood, and now they expected Quick to do the same. Did they not realise how utterly wrong this all felt to her? Did they not feel it too?

'Come on,' Xiaoyu called. She was already inside the little room, waiting.

Quick felt unbalanced by the whole experience, like she was walking on marshmallows, but she followed anyway. As soon as she was inside, Xiaoyu closed the door behind them, sealing them in together. It was a strange space, maybe designed for taking video calls, because although the television screen on the wall was large, the room was filled with a small conference table and six office chairs that were crammed behind it, all facing it. There were office supplies scattered over the centre of the table as though a meeting had just ended: notepads, a pot of pens and other stationery, even a speaker phone.

'Let me take a look at you,' Xiaoyu said, grabbing Quick by the shoulders and squinting at her.

While Xiaoyu assessed her, Quick assessed Xiaoyu. In the short time that had passed since Quick had last seen her, she looked thinner and even more drained. Maybe that was something to do with the contrast between Xiaoyu and Quick's current company, because all the Silver looked so bloody healthy, or maybe it was something to do with the lights up here, but Quick didn't think so.

'You look tired,' Quick said.

Xiaoyu ignored her and asked, 'What's that on your throat?'

'What?' Quick tried and failed to get a look at her own neck.

'It's like two little silvery lines. Let me...' Xiaoyu scooped up Quick's loose hair, pulling it across her back and over her opposite shoulder. Then she leaned in closer. After a second's pause, she grabbed Quick's chin and yanked it down and to one side, then with her other hand she ran her fingers into Quick's hair at the back of her neck, parting it at the base of her skull. 'It's all up in your hair. It looks like you've got silver paint on your scalp, but there's none on your hair. Like it's stained the skin or something. Shit, it's…' She jerked away abruptly, letting Quick's hair fall back into place. 'It's all shiny and weird.'

'Must be a Silver thing, I guess,' Quick said with a shrug. 'I haven't looked in a mirror since… I never really thought about what it would do to me physically. I'm not suddenly going to drop a hundred pounds and start wafting around like an eternally consumptive teenager, am I?'

'I don't think it works like that,' Xiaoyu said. 'The reason they age so slowly is the same reason they heal so quickly: their cells repair themselves as they age or get damaged, by replacing the damaged ones with bits extracted from the blood they drink. Basically, stuff that's broken gets fixed. But fat isn't a defect in your body that gets healed – fat storage is a function your body performs in order to give you reserves in times of need. It's perfectly normal and healthy.'

'Said no doctor to me ever.'

'Well they just did,' said Xiaoyu, her attention back on Quick's neck.

'You're a doctor?' Quick asked.

'Was. Probably won't get the chance to be again. You haven't drunk yet, have you? Blood.'

'What? No. Yes. From a bottle, just after I got turned.'

'But not from the vein.'

'No,' Quick said quietly.

'Well, you're going to have to. If you don't, we're both going to suffer the consequences, and I'm on my last fuck up before gator town.'

'I can't—'

'You'd be surprised how easy the others find it. Just do it before I lose my nerve.'

'If you lose any more blood you're going to fall over.'

'Then I'll sit down,' Xiaoyu said. 'Just get it the fuck over with, will you? Or have you forgotten how much it hurts?'

'I don't want to—'

But Xiaoyu interrupted her by grabbing a pair of scissors from the pot of pens and jamming one of the points into her own wrist, making any further argument impossible. It wasn't just that there was no point in protesting now the blood was already flowing. Instead, Quick's problem was that, with the scent filling the small space, she couldn't hold herself back. She was on Xiaoyu in seconds, pushing the woman down into a chair as she fell to her knees at Xiaoyu's feet and dragged her wrist to her mouth, sucking ravenously.

She hadn't even realised she was hungry.

7

AFTER SPENDING MOST of the day interviewing the new Silver from the block, Kulika was simultaneously bored of talking and horrified by the grief they'd casually shared with her. Each life had been decanted into pills that would be easier for her to swallow, but they all amounted to the same thing in the end: desperation. Everyone came to the mansion in desperation, whether because their need made them easy prey for the Silver or because they came here willingly to escape something worse.

It was more than Kulika had wanted to know.

Looking at the never-ending pool party that was once again gearing up outside the porch, it was so easy to discount these kids as just that: kids. Young people who didn't understand anything about the world or the gravity of their situation, and who only cared about getting wrecked. It was a shallow view, but it was so much easier to believe that than to imagine that these new Silver might have as many terrible reasons for being here as Kulika and her own crew'd had for being on board the *Royal Fortune* three centuries ago. People had thought the pirates were dangerous, immoral, hedonistic raiders, and they had been, but they'd also been terribly damaged people who were each trying to escape whatever haunted them.

You didn't sign up for the precarious, hard-working, perilous world of piracy if you had any other way of making a living. With the picture he painted of unbridled freedom, Bartholomew was remembering it through rose-tinted glasses, though not without some justification. When you were practically immortal, it was truly a life in which there was pleasure to be found, but for the human members of the crew, piracy was a death sentence, sooner or later: scurvy or gangrene or grapeshot or drowning. Believe it or not, in those days most of them couldn't even swim.

It had been worth it, though. Back home they'd had nothing but poverty, starvation, abuse and slavery to look forward to. At least out on the sea, they'd had a chance at making a fortune. That had been enough.

These new Silver were really no different. Some of their incentives to escape were the same, some new. There were more addictions to different drugs, in their families and in themselves, but otherwise Kulika might have been talking to her old crew for all the troubles they shared with her, some more willingly than others.

She was exhausted by it.

All day, and all she had to show for it was a belly full of other people's pain. No one had recognised Evita's name. Most of them knew Jane Doe, but no one knew who had turned her Silver, how she'd come to be at the mansion, or where she'd gone. One day she'd been there, the next not.

The whole thing was an exercise in futility.

It was approaching dark when Kulika finally allowed herself a break. She slipped out onto the porch to find Bayly already there, basking in the evening's heat.

'Party time again,' he muttered into his beer bottle. His

gaze was fixed on the new Silver congregating around the pool.

'Been here all day?' Kulika asked, recalling the last time she'd seen him, in this very same spot that morning with his coffee.

He laughed dryly at that, which she assumed meant no, but with Bayly there was really no telling.

'Heard you got the same bug in your eye as me,' he said.

He meant the silvering, Kulika assumed.

'Seems like,' she said.

'So you're staying.'

It was a statement that didn't need a reply. They both knew that neither of them was going anywhere while the people they loved were still part of Bartholomew's crew.

Forever, probably.

'Strange, that,' Bayly said.

Kulika didn't follow. It wasn't strange to her that she was staying; it felt inevitable.

She looked at Bayly in enquiry.

'It's strange how many new Silver there are here,' he said significantly.

'Yes…' Kulika agreed, but she still wasn't following.

'And back in the old country, I hear. More people silvering too, like you and me.'

It was true: there had been more new Silver in London recently, and more Silver falling irrevocably in love. Before this last year, Kulika couldn't remember hearing about anyone silvering at all, ever. There had always been stories, of course, so she'd known it was technically possible, but it was all so remote that the whole concept had taken on the tone of myth. Maybe it had happened to the friend of a friend of a friend, hundreds of years ago, but never to anyone she actually knew. The fact that it had actually happened to *her...*

Kulika, and Bayly, and that kid Leo who was on the video abducting Cara Alton, and Baron Drake, too. It was like an epidemic.

'Love is in the air,' Bayly said, with a bitter laugh. 'Almost like someone worked out a way to make the turn stick. Chemically.'

That was when Kulika put the pieces together. Enzo working at BioSilver, Enzo joining the crew, then so many new Silver being created at the mansion, and silvering. It was a sequence that started with BioSilver and ended with a Silver army for Bartholomew.

'Enzo took something from the lab,' she guessed.

'Yep.'

Then the implications hit her. 'You mean, me and Quick —'

'Not you,' Bayly interrupted, his tone resentful. 'You don't eat with the crew. Those who do, though.'

'Like you and Enzo.'

'Like us.'

'Fuck, Bayly.'

He nodded. 'Same result, different means. Kind of sours the love connection, though, doesn't it? It's supposed to mean something.'

'It does mean something.'

'Not enough,' Bayly said darkly, looking out towards the horizon, where the Cooper River flowed inexorably to the sea. 'Not when he doesn't feel it, too. It isn't even real.'

'I'm sorry,' Kulika said, because what else was there to say? Bayly was chained to Bartholomew's crew by a love that had been chemically induced.

Forever, probably.

Suddenly, her own situation didn't seem that bad.

'Um, Ms Yadav?' Two of the new Silver were standing at the foot of the porch stairs, looking up at Kulika. 'Monty said you wanted to speak to us?'

The young man was the buccaneer lookalike from the night before, with long, dark hair and an anchor beard. He was dressed colourfully in shorts and a tank top. The young woman wore what looked like pyjamas, as though she'd just been dragged here off the sofa. She had pale skin and long, reddish blonde hair, like a pale imitation of Quick. She was familiar, but Kulika couldn't quite place her.

'All right,' Kulika said, pushing away from the porch railing with little enthusiasm. 'Back to the library, then.'

Bayly nodded in farewell, but he had a look in his eyes that Kulika didn't like: distant, empty, hopeless.

No, she didn't like it one bit.

8

'I'M COMING FOR you,' Quick had told Xiaoyu when she'd finally managed to snap herself out of her bloodlust and relinquish the poor woman's wrist. 'As soon as I can.'

'I'll believe that when I see it,' Xiaoyu had replied.

'I *will*,' Quick had promised.

Xiaoyu had just laughed. There'd been dark circles under her eyes by then, and she'd not been entirely steady on her feet when the others had come to fetch her back to the cellar. She'd been trying to hide it from Quick, but her shoulder still thumped into the doorframe as she left the television room, wobbly and uncontrolled.

Quick felt wretched about it for the rest of the day, but she felt even more wretched now as she lay in bed and tried to imagine how she could have played things differently. She'd never known anything like the complete loss of control that had overwhelmed her when the scent of blood filled the air, not as an adult anyway. She'd felt something like that hunger when she was younger, a starving child left alone in an empty house full of empty cupboards and a padlocked refrigerator. Every time she remembered that feeling, which was constantly now, the shame poured into her stomach and spiralled out through her body in hot curls of horror.

She had to get down into that cellar. She had to know if Xiaoyu was okay, if only for her own peace of mind.

Maybe she could come up with a way of busting all the other humans out of the cellar while she was there, or maybe a quick reconnaissance trip would give her some ideas about how to bust them out later, but that motivation wasn't at the forefront of her mind. All Quick could think as the others finally fell snoring into their beds around her, drunk and messy, was: *Did I kill her?*

Angelina was the last one to sleep. Quick had practically given up waiting for her when the girl stumbled in, jumped straight up from the floor to her top bunk and fumbled the landing in the dark, heedless of the way the impact shook the entire bed frame. If Quick hadn't been awake already, she would have been awakened then.

'Night,' Quick said.

Angelina didn't reply.

Quick was tempted to head down to the cellar right then, but she chose caution instead. Lying back in her bed, she stilled her own breathing and tried to listen for the breathing and heartbeats of the vampires sleeping around her. It was yet another skill they should be able to master, Brandon had told them all, and yet another that had eluded Quick.

It wasn't that she couldn't hear more if she concentrated, because she could. The problem was that letting one sound in meant every other sound came in too, in a rushing cascade at high volume, flooding her brain with so many noises that she couldn't tease them apart. How was she supposed to hear a single heartbeat over the roar of her own? How was she supposed to zero in on a single source from one direction when she was surrounded by cacophony from all around? It was impossible.

After several long, frustrating minutes, Quick gave up trying to be cautious and decided the coast was probably clear. Whatever. She couldn't wait any longer. She slipped out of bed and padded out of the dorm on bare feet.

There were people still partying outside. The stairwell had windows that faced in the direction of the house, and although they were set too high for Quick to see out through them, the eerie blue glow of the pool lights filtered in to illuminate her path. She could hear them, too. There was no music tonight, but there were voices and laughter and the kind of hoots and screams that marked out drinkers who'd gone too far down the bottle to have any volume control. She could only hope that none of them would choose to stagger back this way.

Pausing a moment to make sure the block itself was quiet, Quick padded down the stairs to the bottom floor, and started searching for the cellar hatch. It should have been easy to pinpoint the place, because it wasn't as though she hadn't been there before. The problem was that she'd not been entirely conscious when she'd been dumped down the hatch in the first place, and when she'd come up it had been with a bunch of other humans on their way to be blood donors, so she'd had her mind on other things. She remembered that there'd been a sort of alcove space off the main corridor about twenty feet from the front door, and the hatch was in that alcove, but she couldn't find it now. She was sure the alcove was on the right hand side of the corridor, but there were no doors set in that wall for a clear thirty feet from the main entrance, and the only ones she found led into full rooms. It was the same story on the other side of the corridor.

Quick was bewildered.

Maybe her memory was playing tricks on her. Maybe it

had been a different corridor, next to a different entrance. Or maybe it had been in one of the other wings entirely? Perhaps she could get her bearings better if she came in from the outside, instead of trying to reconstruct her route from the inside out.

She was contemplating this, her hand on the front door, when a bolt of warm air blasted past her, swirling the skirt of her dress and throwing her hair into her face. By the time she'd pulled it back enough that she could see again, she realised she wasn't alone.

Monty and Angelina were standing beside her. Monty had his hand on the door over her own, stopping her from opening it, while Angelina stood behind him looking smug.

'Where are you going?' Monty asked her.

'Outside,' Quick replied.

'Why?'

'Just for some air,' Quick lied, but apparently not very well, because Monty wasn't buying it.

'Oh, Quick, Quick, Quick,' he said sadly, shaking his head.

'Oh, Monty, Monty, Monty,' she parroted back childishly, giving him a dirty look.

He wasn't much impressed with that, either.

'Come on,' he said, grabbing Quick's shoulders and steering her back along the corridor to the big common room. 'I think it's time the two of us had a chat.'

'Monty?' Angelina said sweetly. 'My points?'

'I'll mark them up,' he said over his shoulder. 'Go back to bed.'

'Your bed or mine?'

'Yours,' he said emphatically.

Angelina huffed, then glared at Quick as she stalked past them on her way upstairs.

'What points?' Quick asked Monty.

'There's a hierarchy in the mansion,' he replied, 'and you're fucking up my place in it.' He sat Quick on the nearest sofa, then crouched down in front of her so they were looking at each other eye to eye. 'I was the one who brought you here, so everything you do reflects on me. The fact that the great Kulika Yadav turned you? That works in my favour. The fact that you're being such a giant pain in the ass? That counts against us both.'

'I was just going out for a walk, to look at the stars, you know,' she said.

'No, you weren't,' Monty replied. 'You were looking for the hatch to the cellar.'

Quick's blood ran cold.

'No, I wasn't,' she said.

'Yes, you were. Look, I'm not as stupid as you seem to think I am, and I hear better than pretty much everyone in this block. I know you're planning to break Xiaoyu and the others out, so let me just say: you can't, you won't, and if you try again then shit in here is going to get even hotter for you than it did this morning.'

The memory of fire crawling up her arms made Quick shudder.

'You're crew, now,' Monty went on. 'You don't just get to walk away. You signed the covenant.'

'Yeah, I'm hearing a lot about this covenant,' she replied. 'But I didn't get to read it, or really have any choice about whether or not to sign it, did I? So I'm not sure how you expect me to know what I can and can't do according to it.'

'Then look.' He grabbed her by the arm, dragged her off the sofa and pulled her over to the wall, where a poster-sized laminated list shone in the moonlight that was spilling through the windows. The writing was archaic and incongruous in the context. 'Or let me summarise. No leaving the building without permission. No drinking blood without permission. Do what you're told by your superiors, which to you is everyone.'

'Or?'

'You die,' he said simply.

'I'm a vampire,' Quick replied, confused. 'I'm immortal.'

'No,' Monty replied impatiently. 'You're *Silver*. You're strong, but you can still die, especially when you're this new, and especially if it's other Silver trying to kill you. And trust me, if you break the covenant, the rest of the crew *will* try to kill you. They'll succeed, too.'

'Is that what happened to Evita?' Quick asked quietly.

'*Jane*,' Monty corrected her. 'Her name is *Jane*. And no. I don't know what happened to her, but I'm pretty sure she isn't dead.'

'How do you know?'

Monty looked away and said, 'Just call it a gut feeling.'

'No, Monty,' Quick said irritably. 'I'm going to need more than that.'

'We're looking for her, okay?' he said quietly. 'We want to find her as much as you do.'

Quick looked at him suspiciously, examining his face for the lie. She didn't find one, but she still said, 'I don't believe you.'

'Okay, then don't,' he replied plainly. 'It's not like you can do anything about it either way, sugar.'

'Don't call me sugar.'

'Sugar,' he said antagonistically.

Quick shouldn't have risen to the bait, but she was tired and raw and she couldn't help herself. She swung for his face, but he caught her wrist in his hand and had her pinned facedown on the sofa so quickly that it took her a second or two to understand why she was suddenly lying on her stomach.

'It's that easy for me,' he said, leaning down to whisper into her ear. It felt like he had his knee pressing into the centre of her back, but it could just as easily have been his hand. 'All I have to do is push.' He did, putting enough strain on Quick's ribs that she was certain something was about to snap. 'I can hear your heart thumping, sugar,' he whispered, leaning close as she moaned and struggled for breath. 'That's not a good sign, you know. Just a bit more pressure, maybe a little twist, and I'd crush your heart in your chest.'

'Monty…' she pleaded.

'You think you can't die? That'd be enough, believe me.'

Then the pressure lifted, Monty moved away, and Quick groaned as her strained ribs shifted back into their proper positions. Those seconds of dislocated pain were worse than the pressure itself had been, but they were only seconds. Afterwards, there was no pain at all.

'You made your point,' she breathed, carefully sitting upright.

'Yeah, I did.' He looked at her for a second, then said, 'But you're still not done, are you?'

'I have questions,' she said cautiously. 'All I have is a list of things I'm not supposed to do, but what *am* I supposed to do? Why am I here? Why was Ev— *Jane* here? What's the point of it all?'

Down in the blood cellar, the rules had made a twisted kind of sense. The vampires needed blood, so they imprisoned the humans to provide it for them. They also wanted to turn more people into vampires – *Silver* – and they needed humans for that, too. So far, so sensible.

But what didn't make sense to Quick was why the Silver

would have all these rules for themselves too. Why were they imprisoning themselves? What were they waiting for?

'You don't have to understand,' Monty replied. 'You won't get to understand either, not unless you move up the ladder.'

'You mean like a pyramid scheme? Like a *cult*?'

'Like a *government*,' Monty countered. 'You understand?'

'Not really.'

Monty sighed. 'Go back to bed, Quick.'

'You know I'm sharing a bunk with your new girlfriend, right?'

'Yes.' He closed his eyes and rubbed his temples. 'She did mention it once or twice. And she isn't my girlfriend.' He paused for a moment, then dropped his hands and looked at Quick contemplatively. 'You know,' he said, 'if you don't want to go back to the dorm, you could always come up to my room. We could… talk some more.'

Quick looked at him for a moment, said, 'I think I'd rather sleep with Angelina,' then headed back upstairs to her miserable little bunk.

She still couldn't sleep when she got there, though, and not just because of Angelina's indignant huffing from the bunk above. Her brain wouldn't stop spinning.

Bartholomew and Monty and the others were doing *something* in this place. There was a purpose to all of this, because there must be, and from all that she'd seen it didn't seem possible that their purpose could be good.

Somehow, Evita had escaped it, though. That was enough to give Quick hope.

9

KULIKA COULDN'T SLEEP.

She was fixating on those last two interviews of the day – Brandon and Penny – trying to pull their stories apart in her head and put them back together again in a way that didn't make Bayly look guilty as hell.

There'd been a treasure hunt, of all things. According to Brandon and Penny, they'd been spending a furlough day at one of Charleston's many museums when they'd seen a roster of Stede Bonnet's old crew, and they'd recognised a name: Job Bayly.

He was an idiot to have kept it, really. Kulika was, too, if it came to it. They made fun of Bartholomew – behind his back, of course – for changing his surname all the time, but with the benefit of hindsight, Kulika could see the sense in it. When people tried to trace his history, at least they had to work at it.

Brandon and Penny had already known by then that they were living amongst bona fide pirates, and when they'd made the connection between the gruff man in the mansion and the name on the crew roster, they'd hatched a plan to use Bayly to find Stede Bonnet's pirate gold. Apparently, Jane

Doe had gone along for the ride, at least as far as a cruise ship bound for Jamaica. They'd all boarded separately, each treasure hunter out for themselves, and they'd seen Bayly on board too, but that was where the trail went cold. Brandon and Penny had partied on the ship all the way to the island, poked around Kingston for a day or two without finding anything much, then partied all the way back again. It turned out that Jane – Evita – had been the brains of the operation, which was hardly a surprise given her academic background. Without her, the other two had been entirely at sea.

After they left Jamaica, they'd never seen Jane again. Bayly had already been at the mansion when they returned, and Jane wasn't due home until the end of the week anyway, so they hadn't thought much of it at the time. It was only later, when she missed her curfew, that they began to worry. They should have said something – they both acknowledged that to Kulika – but it turned out that Bayly's reputation was only marginally less scary than her own. When the call had gone out to find Jane, he'd glared, and they'd kept their mouths shut.

Even though it pained them. Even though they felt Jane's absence like a half-forgotten grief in the pits of their stomachs that roused them sweating from their sleep. Bartholomew was right about that: this crew didn't just miss their missing crewmate, they *keened* for her.

After hearing their story, Kulika was conflicted.

There was no pirate gold, of course. There had never been any. They'd collected a lot of plunder in those days, because that's what pirates did, but they'd spent it like water, too. Why bury it in a hole and go hungry when you could have a hot meal and a hot wench every night for as long as it lasted? They hadn't been the kind of people who engaged in sound financial planning. As far as they knew, they'd all be dead before they took the next prize anyway. Might as well make the most of it while they could.

Bayly had been a little different though, hadn't he? A little more secretive than the others, always going off on his own. And then there was Port Royal. He'd haunted that sunken city as much as it had haunted him, always returning as though the ghosts he'd buried there were calling him back.

Kulika had asked about that once, when they'd both been here before. Bayly hadn't told her much, just that the man who'd turned him Silver had been there during the earthquake that swallowed the place whole. He hadn't spelled it out, but Kulika could fill in the gaps: Bayly's maker had died when Port Royal sank.

Was he sad about that? Or relieved? Kulika had never been able to tell either way, which was so often the way it went with Bayly. He felt something, Kulika was sure, but what it was? Only Bayly knew. She hadn't wanted to pry. She'd had her own problems. Still did, but now it looked uncomfortably as though their personal concerns were about to collide.

Maybe it was time she pinned Bayly down and got some answers.

Kulika gave up on sleep, pushed herself out of bed, pulled on her clothes and strode across the room with purpose. But when she reached the door, she found it locked.

What the hell?

She grabbed the handle and rattled it, trying to work out what had gone wrong. When she bent down and squinted through the jamb, she could see that a lock had been thrown on the other side of the door. Several locks, meshing across the threshold to secure the opening, as though she was a wild beast that needed to be caged.

She could have broken the door. Come to that, she could

have just gone out through the window and saved her strength. In the end, she knocked on the connecting door between her rooms and Bartholomew's. If he was going to have the discourtesy to lock her in like an animal, the least she could do in return was interrupt his sleep.

'You locked me in,' she said incredulously when he opened the door.

'No,' he replied, brushing his hair out of sleepy eyes. 'I locked *them* out.'

'*Them* who? The crew?'

'You have some admirers, apparently.'

Kulika stared at Bartholomew, speechless for a moment. 'Why?' she asked eventually.

Bartholomew looked at her quizzically and asked, 'Why not?'

Kulika shook her head, shaking off the irrelevancy, and said, 'I need to speak to Bayly. Now.'

Bartholomew was quiet for a moment, tipping his ear towards the floor as though he could hear straight down to Bayly's room on the storey below. Maybe he could, because the next thing he said was, 'He's not here.'

'What? Where is he?'

'He'll be back tomorrow,' Bartholomew assured her. 'They'll all be back tomorrow.' From the tone of his voice, it was clear there was an implication in those words that Kulika didn't understand.

'What's tomorrow?' she asked. 'Is this about Cara Alton?'

Bartholomew laughed. 'It's never been *about* her,' he said. 'She's just a tool. You'll see, tomorrow.'

'Can't you just tell me? If you want me to support you, don't you need me to know—'

'Tomorrow,' he said, turning to face her, which effectively stopped her from following him. 'I'll send for you.'

Kulika didn't want to wait until tomorrow. She wanted to follow up on every piece of information she had immediately, so she could find Evita Khalyed and bring her back here to Quick and the crew—

No. Bring her back for *Dr Ross*, so she could save Baron Drake and Jack.

Right?

Either way, the end result would be the same, and her mission hadn't changed: find Evita Khalyed. It was simple. She didn't need to let Bartholomew make it complicated.

'I know you're impatient,' he said, 'but it's late, and you need to rest. And before you do that, I need you to make a call.'

'A call?' Kulika asked, thrown. 'Who am I calling?'

'Your old mansion.'

'My old…'

'It'll be morning there by now.'

She'd stayed up so late that it was tomorrow, and it would be later still back in Oxford.

'I'll see you at breakfast,' Bartholomew said, then he smiled encouragingly at her before closing the connecting door between them. He didn't lock it, though, because he didn't need to lock himself away from Kulika. Not now he had her on such a short leash.

Kulika stood there for a moment, staring at the door. Then she crossed the room, pulled her phone out of her back pocket, and lay down on the bed.

Bartholomew was right, of course. She had to make the call. Kulika might not have any numbers stored in her phone, but fortunately she knew Baron Drake's office number by heart.

'Hello?' he answered on the second ring. Even with the time difference, it was still early enough in Oxford that the

Baron wouldn't normally have been at his desk.

'It's Kulika,' she said.

'You've seen the news, I suppose,' he said, with the kind of exhaustion in his voice that suggested there'd been no rest for him since it broke. Probably not since long before then. Without the antidote Evita Khalyed's blood would provide, Jack was getting closer to death every day, along with Baron Drake himself. 'Bartholomew's work?' he asked.

'Yes.'

'And he's listening in?'

'Safest to assume that, yeah.'

'Then I'll keep it brief. The Primus is… No. I'll keep it briefer: find Evita Khalyed and come home.'

'I'm working on the first part. The second might be harder to swing.'

'Kulika—'

'What I'm saying is that it might be a good idea to get Dr Ross out here,' Kulika interrupted, 'if you can spare her. Then she can bring her formula with her and take what she needs from Dr Khalyed's blood the moment I track her down. That way, you won't have to rely on me to bring the antidote back for you if I'm… delayed.'

He paused for a beat, then said, 'Should I send Hugo?'

'No,' Kulika said quickly.

Adding more of the baron's people into the mix wouldn't help at this point. She was going to have a hard enough time extracting the doctor when the time came without having to worry about anyone else.

The doctor would have to come, though. There was no getting around that. Kulika was certain that, even if she did manage to find Evita Khalyed, Bartholomew wouldn't let the girl leave the mansion any more than he'd let Kulika herself leave. After all, they were both crew.

'All right,' the baron said. 'I'll send her. When?'

'I'll be in touch.'

'Make it soon.'

'I'll do my best,' she replied, but he'd already hung up.

Kulika hated to put Dr Ross in danger, but if the doctor had proved anything over the past year, it was that she could look after herself. Besides, this was the best plan available in the circumstances. If Khalyed couldn't go to the doctor, then the doctor was going to have to come to Khalyed, then take the antidote back to Oxford, leaving Kulika behind.

This was the truth that Kulika knew in her gut: by bribery or by choice, she would be at Bartholomew's side from now until the end of it all.

However soon that day might come.

10

IT WAS LATE on Sunday morning, the atmosphere sticky and hot, before Quick and the rest of the dorm finally woke from their exhausted sleep. When they did, they woke dramatically.

First there was a crash and a scream, a couple of bunks away from Quick's. Then a splatter of something wet and warm hit her face. By the time she'd sat up and rubbed the liquid away with her sleeve, the whole room had descended into chaos. She saw the colour on her sleeve: blood red.

'Holy crap!' someone yelled.

'Fire!' yelled someone else, then everyone was hopping out of their beds and thundering towards the dormitory door in a single, unrestrained mass. They were bunched around the doorway, kicking and clawing as they tried to get past each other.

Quick looked towards the window at the other end of the dorm, which was currently aflame, trying to find another way out. That was when she noticed that the man in the bottom bunk next to hers wasn't moving. His sheets were starting to char around him, the result of an unbroken Molotov cocktail that sat smouldering on his pillow, but still he didn't move. There was something wrong with his head. In the spot above his ear, where there should have been tight, short braids of dark hair to match the ones covering the rest of his scalp, there was a long furrow of white, pink and red. No wonder he wasn't moving.

Quick should have run with the others. She should have just got out. The fire was raging around the window and the room had already filled with smoke. Besides, she didn't know these people, and they'd shown little enough consideration for her – and each other – that surely she didn't owe them anything. But the man's sheets were starting to burn properly now, and Quick couldn't help but think back to her sun-related accident on the training field yesterday. She knew how it felt to have fire licking up your limbs, and that gave her a pang of sympathy for the man who was probably already dead.

Only probably, though. The whisper of a chance was enough to have her dragging the sheets off her bed to smother the flames on his, then dragging his inert body off his own bed and towards the door. By that point, it wasn't crowded anymore. From what Quick could see through the smoke, it looked as though the others had disappeared entirely.

'Someone give me a hand, here!' she yelled into the thick air, but no one called back. All she could hear was crackling and roaring as the fire took hold behind her. With so many Silver in the building with extraordinary powers, could they really not organise a bucket chain?

Which is when she remembered: she had those powers too. Allegedly. She had yet to activate any of them successfully, but didn't people always say that you could do amazing things when fuelled with adrenaline? If humans could lift cars off human children, then surely Quick could carry one unconscious Silver out of a burning building.

And maybe she would have done, had it not been for bloody Monty.

Quick was halfway down the block's many stairs with the unconscious man slung over her shoulder when Monty rushed up from the ground floor and nearly knocked her flat.

'Leave him!' he yelled at her over the sound of the roaring fire.

'No!' Quick yelled right back at him.

'You're going to get yourself killed!'

'You're going to get *him* killed!' she said, shrugging her shoulder to indicate the man she was carrying with surprising ease. But then the smoke caught in her lungs. Brandon had told them yesterday that they didn't technically need to breathe anymore, but Quick's body disagreed. She started coughing and she couldn't stop, every heaving breath dragging more toxic particles into her lungs so that she had to cough again, then heave in another breath, in a terrible endless loop. It didn't stop until Monty flung her over one shoulder and the man over the other, then carried them both outside to the training ground. Quick made sure to keep to the shade.

'He'll live,' Monty said, dumping the unconscious man onto the ground.

'We've got to get the others out,' Quick said, turning to go back into the building. 'There are hundreds of people in the cellar, and if we don't open the hatch they'll all—'

'They're fine,' Monty said, looking unconcerned. In fact, as she looked around the crowd that had gathered outside the block, Quick noticed that no one looked particularly concerned. Some of them were even heading back inside, as though Quick hadn't just barely staggered out.

'What—'

'Fire's out,' one of the others said as they walked past Quick. 'Two minutes forty three. Looks like one of the bottles didn't smash, so I'm docking you twenty points.'

'*Twenty*?' the woman next to him said incredulously.

'You're still a hundred and ten up on the day. Just take the win.'

Quick looked at Monty, expecting an explanation, but he avoided her eyes, then walked off as soon as he spotted Angelina.

Quick looked down at her ragged cotton dress, now stained with blood and soot to add to the general dirtiness it had already acquired. She grabbed a handful of her hair and sniffed it: charred plastic and grease.

'What the hell was that?' she asked no one in particular.

'Fire drill,' Bella said with a shrug. 'If you want to move up the board, maybe next time don't stop to drag out a corpse.'

'What board?' Quick asked, but Bella had walked away too, heading back inside the building.

Quick followed her, in search of answers. It seemed like most of the crowd was heading the same way now, filing towards the big common room. But instead of gathering at the end nearest to the doors, where Brandon had been holding the humans the day before, everyone was clustered instead around the large television on the wall at the far end of the room, the one that showed the list Quick had noticed previously. As she got closer, she saw it was a list of names next to a load of numbers she couldn't parse. It scrolled down, the numbers changing, flicking red and green as they went up and down, apparently controlled by a young woman hunched over a laptop beneath the screen.

'Plus twenty for mine!' a guy yelled. 'She came out first.'

'No, mine did,' a woman argued back.

'Twenty each,' Monty said, pushing to the front of the crowd. 'And ten for each sire.'

The numbers changed, and the names and lines shuffled up and down the board.

'Hundred and ten for me,' someone else shouted, the woman Quick had seen outside. 'Duke agreed.'

'Fine,' said Monty, and again the board shifted and updated.

There were a few more shouted numbers, and a few more adjustments from the woman on the laptop, but by that time Quick wasn't paying attention anymore, because she'd worked out what the screen actually was.

They were *ranks*, like this was some kind of gameshow, and not just for the newcomers. Everyone was on the screen somewhere. As the list was finalised and began to scroll in a continuous loop from top to bottom, Quick saw Monty's name in the very first slot: Angel Monteiro. That explained why he was suddenly swaggering around like he owned the place. She couldn't find Kulika's name, though, not anywhere.

Quick's was easy enough to spot, though.

'You started off at the top of the newbies,' said Penny, coming up beside her. 'But the others crept up on points yesterday when you couldn't do Silver speed or jumping, and you actually lost points today because Monty had to rescue you from the fire.'

'I lost more points than the guy I pulled out of there?' Quick said incredulously.

'Well, you made some pretty stupid choices. Kaiden just had the misfortune to get hit in the head with a Molotov cocktail, which wasn't really his fault. So, yeah. You're coming in dead last.'

'I don't understand,' Quick said, looking at the scrolling

board as though she could decipher the deeper meaning behind it if she simply squinted harder. 'They set our dorm on fire to win *points*?'

'This place is boring,' Penny said, as though that were explanation enough.

'Excuse me?'

'We're out in the middle of Bumfuck South Carolina, and there's nothing to do. Playing with the board passes the time, and it means fewer arguments in the long run. Trust me. I was here in January, back before they put it up, and it was fucking awful.'

'*This* is awful,' Quick said, horrified. 'That guy nearly died.'

'Yeah, but at least he was the only one. People used to get into death matches every hour, fighting over who got first pick from the blood cellar, or who got the nicest bunk. Petty shit, but then petty shit feels big when there's nothing to distract you from it. This way, we always know who's on top.'

Quick felt sick about the whole thing. The board wasn't based on merit. Instead, from the little she'd seen, the people who topped the pack were the ones who were the best at behaving like dicks, either because they were the strongest or because they came up with stupid pranks like setting the dorm on fire. If those were the requirements to succeed in this place, then Quick was going to fail miserably.

But she was stuck here. Last night had made that abundantly clear.

'I guess I'm screwed, then,' Quick muttered.

'Oh, don't be like that,' Penny replied. Quick hadn't been talking to her, but Penny didn't seem to realise that. 'You won't get up to the top, but if you worked at it you could hit close enough to the middle to earn some privileges at least.'

Quick's interest sharpened. 'Like what?' she asked.

'Like more blood, better food, better rooms.'

'Showers?'

'What?' Penny screwed up her pretty little nose. 'Don't tell me you've been mouldering in that dirty dress since the Casting ceremony?'

The disgust in her voice just made Quick angry.

'No one told me I had another option! I thought we had to get permission for everything around here.'

'And you didn't think it was weird that everyone else was wearing clean clothes?'

'How was I supposed to know that? It's not like any of them actually talk to me,' Quick said, her temper snapping. Then she added sulkily, 'None of them came here from the blood cellar. I just thought they'd been wearing better things when they arrived.'

But now she came to think about it, Quick realised that the dresses and suits and swimwear had been replaced over the course of the past day with more practical clothing. It was just that she'd been concentrating on other things. She might have been around the others nonstop since the Casting, but she'd been pretty much alone the whole time.

Penny's expression softened along with her tone. 'You're not in the cellar anymore. You can shower whenever you like. Get new clothes from the wardrobe, too, and there's always something to eat in the kitchen, even if it's crap. The board's just for the big ticket items like dinner with the captain, furlough for trips off the property. Stuff like that.'

'We *are* stuck here, then?'

'Not forever.' Penny smiled awkwardly. 'But I'd be lying if I said people don't get points for hunting down deserters.'

Shit.

How was she ever going to get herself and Xiaoyu out of

here, or find Evita, if she had power-hungry Silver dogging her every move?

Quick thought for a moment, then asked, 'How high do you need to get for the big-ticket things?'

'Dinner with the captain? Top ten, I'd say. The rest, top half maybe? Look, don't worry about it. You'll get there. Just go get cleaned up, all right? Today's a big day.'

Quick wanted to ask what that meant, but everyone was leaving the common room now that the board had been updated. Penny slipped away with them, leaving Quick with a lot to consider.

She took her time in the shower, and in the wardrobe afterwards, mulling things over as she did so. There was another matter of concern, too: when Quick checked her neck in the bathroom mirror, there was no silver on it or – as far as she could see – at the base of her skull. Had Xiaoyu been mistaken yesterday, or was she losing it? Either way, Quick couldn't leave her down in the cellar much longer without checking on her. She had to find a way out, and she had to do it fast.

In the wardrobe, Quick chose clothes that would cover as much of her skin as possible, whilst also being light enough for the heat and sturdy enough to work out in. When she returned to the dorm, at first she thought she'd walked into the wrong room. There was no blood, no ash, no fire damage at all. She walked back out and realised there was no damage in the corridor either, even though the whole building had been filled with ink-black smoke half an hour before.

It was unsettling, to say the least.

There was a bottle of sunscreen on her bed, along with a parasol. An actual parasol. It had a wooden handle, and the frame was covered with black material and trimmed with lace. It looked *quaint*. Quick was not quaint. She would never be quaint, but apparently she was about to spend the day leaping and running around the training ground looking like Mary fucking Poppins.

'Hurry up, newbie!' someone yelled from down the hall.

Quick didn't realise it was her they were yelling at until an angry woman popped her head around the doorway of the dorm and said, 'Hey, newbie! Get your ass in here!'

'Excuse me?' said Quick.

'You're bottom twenty on the board, am I right? Well, *bottom* bottom.'

'Yes…'

'Then you're on clean up duty. Did no one tell you?'

'I… No, I—'

'Then *hurry up*. You're already late, so if you could get any lower on the board, you already would be. If you want to earn any points at all today, you'll shift it! Now!'

Quick obeyed.

In the dorms further along the corridor, people were scrubbing and painting and replacing furniture, some at Silver speed and some at the only speed Quick could manage. Someone gave her a paintbrush and pointed her at a section of stripped wall. No one spoke, they just worked with the kind of concentration that told her they were serious about getting more points for the board.

Over the course of the morning, Quick realised she should get serious too.

Furlough for trips off the property, Penny had said.

Off the property.

Which gave Quick a new objective: get up the bloody board, and do it fast.

11

THE MANSION WAS busy this morning. Kulika had woken to the noises of engines in the driveway, furniture being moved in the rooms below hers, and laughter in the hallways. It was as if the crew was congregating for Sunday church. Kulika wasn't sure she'd like the object of their worship.

Frustratingly, Bayly was not amongst the newly-returned crew. She'd checked the porch, where he would normally be drinking his coffee, and found it empty. She'd checked his room on the floor below hers, and found only a stripped single bed surrounded by no personal effects at all.

That was when she really began to panic.

'Bartholomew,' she said, pushing her way into the library without an invitation. 'Where's Bayly? You said he'd be back today.'

'No,' Bartholomew said, slowly rising from his desk chair. 'I said he'd be back tonight.'

'You said today.'

'Tonight is today. Either way, I don't think it's enough of an emergency to justify this intrusion. Do you?'

It was only then that Kulika realised they weren't alone in

the room. Monty was on his knees at the far end of the room, his face pointed into the corner of the bookshelves like a naughty child paying penance for talking in class.

'What's going on?' she asked.

'Oh, nothing,' Bartholomew said, walking around the desk to join Kulika at the door. 'Just a little misunderstanding about fire safety. Walk with me, won't you?'

Kulika glanced at Monty, still motionless in the corner, then looked uncertainly back at Bartholomew. 'All Bayly's things are gone from his room,' she said. 'I don't think he's coming back, and I need to talk to him now.'

'Oh, he's coming back,' Bartholomew promised her. 'Don't you worry about that. Now, come with me.'

Reluctantly, Kulika let herself be led to the door at the far end of the mansion's kitchen, the one she'd followed Bartholomew to the other day after the unlucky Alex came home. He opened it to reveal a set of brick stairs leading down into a space lit with bare, dim bulbs. From the doorway, Kulika could see nothing except the corner in the stairwell below them where the steps turned to the side, leading down deeper.

She didn't want to go down.

'What are you showing me?' she asked, trying not to sound as hesitant as she felt.

'Part two of the grand revelation plan,' Bartholomew said with a smile, then he stepped up close behind her, forcing her to move down the steps so she didn't end up falling down instead. He shut the door behind them.

Kulika turned to look where she was going, resigning herself to the descent. She took a step, and another, and with each one the temperature dropped so perceptibly that she was sure the space must have been artificially cooled. But there were no wires, no hum of air conditioning, nothing except the bare wires tacked to the walls, trailing power to the bulbs above their heads as they descended into the frigid space below.

She'd never been down here in the bad old days, but then she'd never gone into the kitchen at all. The old cook would have thrown his meat cleaver at her. He'd been precious about his domain. Besides, they all knew Bartholomew had buried things under the mansion, things both living and dead. No one went underground except him, not just because it was forbidden, but because only an idiot would go digging up the skeletons Bartholomew had accumulated over five hundred years of sin. Some secrets are best left buried.

'What is this place?' she asked.

'Cold storage,' Bartholomew said, with an edge of amusement in his tone that chilled Kulika's blood.

She suspected she wasn't going to enjoy the joke. Her suspicion was confirmed when she turned the corner and saw the body laid out on a large stone plinth raised up from the centre of the dirt floor.

'Leo, I presume?' she asked, breathing through her mouth.

She could smell the rot from here. It might have been cool in the cellar, but they were still in South Carolina in high summer, and the poor kid had been dead five days. There was only so much that could be done to preserve a body without the benefits of proper refrigeration and embalming fluid.

'Tell me you're not going to eat him,' she added, her upper lip curling back involuntarily.

'Not all of him,' Bartholomew replied, stepping past her on the stairs so he could circle the plinth. 'Jessamy knows her work well. When she and Alex went to find Leo, she drained and chilled his blood before arranging to transport him back here. Poor Alex,' Bartholomew added, shaking his head sadly as though he wasn't the one who'd incited his execution. 'The blood may not be entirely fresh, but it's fresh enough for the Convocation.'

'The Convocation?'

'Tonight,' Bartholomew said with a gleeful smile that made Kulika uneasy. 'You'll see.'

'This is the thing you wouldn't tell me about yesterday,' she guessed. 'This is why everyone's coming back to the mansion today.'

'Exactly. Think of it as a crew meeting, where the old guard will have a chance to welcome the newcomers. And what a meeting it will be. We're celebrating, Kulika,' Bartholomew said. His joy felt out of place in the cellar that had become a crypt. 'The number of Silver we created on Friday night was unprecedented. *Unprecedented.* Not in all his years as Primus, and god king, and whatever else he wants to hold himself out to be, did Solomon achieve anywhere near the numbers we're pulling in. Do you have any idea how long it's been since Silver were made and gathered in a single group the size of our current crew?'

'No,' Kulika said. She still thought it was reckless to leave so many new Silver practically unsupervised, but she knew this wasn't the moment to say so. Bartholomew was in speech mode now, and all he wanted was for her to play along with the call and response.

'Never,' he said. '*Never*, not in all the millennia the Silver have been walking the earth. We're a new breed, and we're stronger than any Silver that have come before us.'

Kulika didn't like the way this was going. She'd heard that kind of talk before, and she knew just how insidious could be. Hearing yourself talked about in those terms made you feel special, a blessed part of the elite. It might even make you feel sorry for the people who weren't so fortunate, in the beginning at least, but once you heard it often enough you'd slip into disdain and start to feel that your specialness entitled you to more than those who were not like you. After all, weren't you *worth* more than them? Weren't you better? Once you became nicely embedded in those ideas, it was just a slow, incremental slide towards thinking that the world would be better off if it didn't contain anyone who wasn't as special as you.

In Bartholomew's words, Kulika could hear the first wave of the storm that would sink the ship.

'And then there's this,' he said, crossing the cellar to a second, sheet-covered plinth Kulika hadn't noticed before, because it was tucked into an alcove like a sarcophagus would be in a crypt.

'Cara Alton?' Kulika asked.

'The very same.'

'But why bring her back here? She's not crew.'

'No, but that doesn't mean she can't be useful to us,' he said. 'You know the old stories about silvering, I suppose?' He walked the length of the plinth slowly as he spoke, trailing his fingertips along the covered body like he was a car salesman tempting Kulika with a shiny new Porsche.

'I know some.'

'Well, a lot of them are fantasy, obviously. There's this romanticised idea that when the person a bonded Silver loves dies, the life bond disintegrates that Silver into a pile of twinkling dust and they just… blow away on the breeze. To counter that ridiculous theory—' Bartholomew turned and gestured expansively at Leo's very solid, un-dusty corpse. '—I present Exhibit A.'

'And your point is?'

'My point is that although some of the myths are hokum, not all of them are. Which brings me to Exhibit B.'

He ripped the sheet off Cara Alton's body with gratuitous drama, the material snapping through the air like a whip. The poor girl was half-naked underneath it, her skirt bunched up around her hips, her T-shirt pushed up to reveal her bare stomach. Bare, that is, except for the silver handprint that glimmered on her stomach.

'You know what that is?' Bartholomew asked in a low voice.

He must have seen the silver mark Kulika had left on Quick's neck when she'd healed her bite. It wasn't worth denying that she recognised the peculiar shine, glinting like frozen mercury beneath Cara Alton's skin.

'It's a healing mark,' she said.

'Wrong,' he replied with a grin, pleased that she'd remained on-script. 'It's the straw that's going to break the camel's back. The sceptics can dismiss the Silver speed video as doctored or fake, but when they have this girl's body? When they open her up and look at what's inside her, do you know what they're going to find?'

'No.'

'Nothing,' he said emphatically. 'No blood, no exit wound through which the blood could have been drawn, and an indelible silver mark that's penetrated the skin far deeper than any stain would go. It'll be on her cells, you know. It goes right down to the bone, a mark like that.' He smiled as though he were remembering something funny, then said, 'I opened one of them up once. Even the *blood* was silver.'

A sharp rush of fear skittered across Kulika's skin.

'Not our Patience,' Bartholomew said with a laugh. 'You'd know if it had been her. You'd feel it, the way *he* felt it when I— But I'm becoming distracted, aren't I?'

Bartholomew's smile did nothing to reassure her, but then it wasn't intended to. It was intended as a threat.

Then the smile softened, and Kulika was left wondering if she'd imagined the menace she'd seen in it just a moment before.

'I want you beside me tonight,' he said, taking her hand in his. 'For the Convocation.' His words felt sincere, but Kulika could no longer follow the emotional thread of their conversation. Was this an order, or a request? Was he threatening to hurt Quick if she didn't, or had he genuinely been sharing a twisted memory with her and expecting her to appreciate it? Given her history, that wasn't beyond the realms of possibility, but she no longer had any idea of Bartholomew's angle.

Perhaps *that* was the intention.

'Is this a test?' she asked suspiciously.

'Call it an offer,' he said.

'An offer of what?'

'Just be ready when I come for you at midnight,' he said.

On the off-chance that it was neither test nor offer, but threat, Kulika resolved to make sure that she was waiting.

There had been no sign of Bayly all day. Instead, Kulika had spent her time talking to all the returning Silver to discover what they knew about Dr Evita Khalyed, AKA Jane Doe. She'd been hoping to find something – anything – to point her away from Bayly, but the returning Silver knew even less than the Silver from the block. Most of them didn't even remember "Jane", beyond the tugging ache that her absence created in each of them.

That, it seemed, was more real to them than Evita herself had been.

All too soon it was midnight, and Bartholomew appeared at her door with a robe in his arms and a smile on his lips, neither of which seemed like good signs. Still, Kulika followed him downstairs into the candlelit silence of the hall, where hundreds of other robed Silver waited for them.

This time, Bartholomew didn't stop at the mezzanine, not like he had done at the Casting. Instead, he led Kulika right down to the foot of the staircase, where he stood and addressed his crew.

Their crew.

'Tonight is the last night that we'll come together like this in darkness,' he said, holding his robed arms open wide like a priest inviting them all to take the sacrament. 'The next time we gather, the Convocation will be in daylight, in the open, and we will no longer need to hide our power. In anticipation of that revelation, I'm making a revelation of my own.' He paused dramatically, then turned slightly towards Kulika and added, 'I trust that my Second requires no introduction.' The gesture was enough to make his meaning clear.

Half of the crew had already seen Kulika with Bartholomew since her return, at the Casting ceremony if not at the demise of Alex, and it didn't seem to surprise any of the new Silver that she'd been returned to her former position, no more than it surprised Kulika herself.

He gives and he takes.

But the older Silver in the congregation *were* surprised, though their shock at Bartholomew's words had less to do with her elevation than it did with the title he'd given her.

Second.

The Latin word for that was *Secundus*, the name given to the Primus's second-in-command.

No wonder the older Silver were shocked. Some of them were as old as Bartholomew himself, and they'd see the title he'd given Kulika as an indicator of his own intentions. America had never ascribed to the rule of Solomon, or to any of the other Primi around the world who pretended they were his peers, but now Bartholomew was using the language of the Silver kings.

That couldn't have been unintentional. Every single thing Bartholomew did was deliberate. He had the power already, and now it seemed he was snatching the title too. He was setting himself up as a new Primus.

Despite their shock, not one of the convocants objected.

Bartholomew looked around the Convocation, assessing their reactions. No one was stupid enough to show him anything but acceptance, not amongst the crew.

Later, though.

Kulika wondered about later.

There was a table placed at the foot of the staircase and off to one side, tucked slightly behind the banisters, so Kulika hadn't noticed it at first. Bartholomew walked over to it now and lifted from it the most ornate cup Kulika had ever seen. It was a large and fierce thing, double-handled and rounded at the bottom like a bowl. Between the two handles, looping over the top of the vessel like an arched bridge between its two edges, was a curved blade. There was something odd about the inside of the bowl too, because when Bartholomew took it in his hands, his face was suddenly illuminated from below, as though the mirrored surface were concentrating and directing the light from all the meagre candles that lit the hall and turning them into more than the sum of their parts. It felt like a religious item, a cup that really deserved to be called a chalice.

Seeing its construction, Kulika had a pretty good idea what it was for.

Bartholomew passed it to the first Silver on his left, holding it reverently by both handles as he lowered the base into the man's palms. Now that his face was illuminated by the inside of the cup, Kulika saw that it was Monty. He didn't mess around. He brought the wrist of his free hand right down onto the curved blade, opened the vein so it bled a little into the bowl, then shifted his grip to hold the cup by both handles as he passed it to the next person in line. By the time it had made its way halfway around the hall, the light reflecting up from the inside of the bowl was distinctly dimmed, and the entire outside of the cup was darkened and dirtied with smeared blood.

Then it came into Quick's hands.

Kulika had been aware of her since the minute she walked in the door. How could she not be? Every gesture Quick made, every tiny shift of her clothing, sent her perfume rolling in waves across the hall to Kulika. She could feel her nostrils flaring, desperately trying to catch every facet and intricacy of Quick's scent, but she couldn't stop it. She didn't *want* to stop it. With the kaleidoscopic aroma filling her head, Kulika was transported back to that kiss, that bite, and away from this dark cabal.

When Quick opened her vein into the cup with a hesitant grimace, Kulika felt the pain as though it had sliced through her own wrist. She smelled the blood too, and it sparked a protective fury in her stomach that she hadn't expected. She wanted to rush across the hall and knock the cup from Quick's hands. She wanted to pull Quick's wrist to her mouth and heal her wound, but then everyone would know that Kulika had silvered for her. Given her new status as Bartholomew's Second and all the competition that would provoke, it seemed ill-advised to advertise the fact that bumping off just one vulnerable new Silver – Quick – would be enough to take out Kulika too.

Stupid.

Seeing Quick bleeding across the hall, there was nothing

Kulika could do about it except watch and worry and yearn.

'Steady,' Bartholomew whispered to her, so softly that she imagined she would be the only one to hear it.

It shouldn't have worked.

One word, and from *him*.

He touched her hand, and the word spread through her body like a command.

Steady.

It really shouldn't have worked.

Nonetheless, the fury rushing through Kulika's body settled immediately. Her fists unclenched, her jaw relaxed, and she couldn't even smell the blood so much anymore. It was as though Quick's scent had dissipated into the air, banished at a single word, a single touch from Bartholomew.

Perhaps it was just conditioning from all those long years serving beneath his flag. Either way, Kulika didn't like it, and she was riling herself up to get angry about it, but then Bartholomew released her hand with a smile and the world came rushing back in. By then, the danger was gone. Quick had passed the cup on to the next Silver, who started the whole grim business up again. Round and round the circle, until the cup returned to them, full now.

Bartholomew took the cup and put it back on the table, next to a stoppered vial Kulika hadn't noticed before.

'Our crewmate, Leo,' he said, raising the vial up high before emptying its contents into the cup and swirling it around. Next, he held the cup out towards Kulika and nodded at the blade. Reluctantly, she cut herself on it and contributed her own blood. Finally, Bartholomew cut his own wrist and added his blood to the mix, then sent the cup around the hall again.

This time, they all drank, Quick included. There was no way for Kulika to intervene, and no good reason that she should. After all, it was just a little blood. What could it hurt?

She wondered then whether Bartholomew had been deliberately trying to emulate a religious event. It was fitting, because here they were taking communion, only the blood was their own, and Bartholomew's. For a girl born when Kulika had been, raised to be a good Catholic, there was a twisted and solipsistic symbolism in it that crept unpleasantly into her mind.

Bartholomew didn't drink, she noticed, so Kulika didn't either. When the cup reached her, she turned to offer Bartholomew the nearly-drained vessel instead. His gaze lingered on hers as their hands met around it, and for a moment she thought he was going to hold it up to her lips, but instead he just held her fingers in place beneath his so she couldn't let go of the cup.

He was waiting for something, and Kulika had a terrible suspicion that she knew what it was. *This* was the test.

'Your chalice, Primus,' she said, loudly enough that her voice rang out across the hall.

Bartholomew smiled his approval and released her hands, then turned to place the cup down on the table behind him.

The candles snuffed out, the ceremony apparently over. The crew departed quickly and quietly after that, leaving Kulika and Bartholomew alone in the dark.

'How do you do that?' she asked him, feeling grateful and violated all at the same time. 'The way you steadied me like that.'

'I made you, Kulika,' he said plainly. 'Blood calls to blood.'

Kulika didn't know how to feel about that, or what it meant for the ceremony she'd just witnessed. Taken part in, even. It didn't sound good, though. It sounded like

Bartholomew had an influence over her that she'd never fully appreciated.

'I could do more than just that for you,' he went on, 'if you'd only drink.'

'From that?' Kulika asked, looking askance at the dirty, bloody cup.

'Or from a purer source,' Bartholomew said, offering his healed wrist to her.

It was one hell of an offer. The Silver didn't drink each others' blood, not under normal circumstances. It was done only when new Silver were made, or in dire straits when a Silver was injured and there was no other blood available, or if the Silver were in a sexual relationship and were feeling kinky. The Convocation tonight had been irregular enough, but the offer Bartholomew had just made to Kulika?

It was intimate enough that it probably went against his vow of celibacy.

'I can't accept that,' Kulika replied, backing up a little. If he could settle her with a word and a touch through the connection his blood had forged between them three hundred years ago, what control would he gain over her if she accepted now?

'I would allow your lips on my skin, Kulika,' he said softly.

'And what would you demand of me in return?' she asked. *He gives and he takes.*

He smiled and pulled the sleeve of his robe back down over his wrist. 'Not tonight, then. Later, perhaps.'

'Perhaps,' Kulika said, while silently vowing to herself that it would be *never*.

'You did well tonight. In fact, I think you've earned a little trust.'

Then he took her hand in his, raised it to his lips, and

finally delivered the words of benediction she'd been waiting for.

12

THE SILVER OF the block were partying. Quick hadn't earned the right to join them yet, Monty told her, but since this was a special night – the Convocation to end all others – the top rankers were willing to make an exception.

'Do we have to?' someone asked Monty as they passed on their way to the pool.

Belatedly, Quick realised it was Kaiden.

She was a little surprised to learn that he was now amongst the top rankers, but not as surprised as she was by his attitude towards her. She'd saved his life. She'd got herself demoted on the stupid board to drag his body out of a burning building and not only did he not seem particularly grateful, he seemed to be actively resenting her help. Quick hadn't expected effusive thanks or anything – to her mind, she'd only done what any decent human being would do in the same circumstances – but then they weren't human anymore, were they? Rules of common decency no longer applied.

Kaiden's attitude didn't make the invitation to the pool party any more appealing. Quick felt out of place and useless so, not being the type of person who was inclined to accept a bad hand without drawing again to see if she could get something better, she made some desultory excuses to Monty, then dragged herself outside to the training ground to try the running and jumping drills again.

After an hour, it wasn't going well. Her stomach was roiling, but she couldn't tell whether that was because she was hungry, or because she was feeling sick from the blood cocktail she'd drunk at the Convocation. Just a sip, as she'd been instructed, but still, she was beginning to regret drinking it at all. She hadn't been given a choice, but then she probably wouldn't have refused even if she had been, because of the stupid board. Despite her connection to the apparently-famous and ever-absent Kulika Yadav, she was still on the bottom.

Kulika hadn't been absent tonight, though, had she? She'd been right there next to Bartholomew. She'd probably been at the mansion this whole time, only Quick wasn't allowed to leave the block to see her and Kulika apparently had no inclination to come and see her. Quick had thought – naively, she now realised – that it meant something that Kulika had come to rescue her yesterday. She'd even imagined – naively again – that she might have Kulika on her side when she came to make her daring escape, however she managed it.

No such luck. She was on her own, which meant there was only one course of action she could follow: she needed points. If she wanted to be given enough leeway to find Evita, free Xiaoyu, and get them all the hell out of here, she needed more status than she had right now. Otherwise, she was going to spend every day in the block like she had spent today: painting the walls, cleaning the toilets, carrying supplies, and generally tiring herself out so much that even on the rare occasions that she was allowed a blood ration to regain her strength, she'd be too exhausted to do anything but sleep.

That was another reason she'd chosen to come out to the training ground and practice rather than party the night away: this might be the only chance she'd get to score some points for her abilities.

If only she could get a single bloody one of them to work.

As Quick was trying and failing for the hundredth time to jump more than a foot in the air, a voice said, 'Let me try,' from the sidelines.

Quick thought she recognised the voice, but she didn't believe that Kulika was really there until she turned around and saw her leaning up against the wall of the block, watching. Her robes were gone now. She was dressed in dark trousers and a black racer-back top that bared her arms and showed every muscled inch of her shoulders.

Quick said, 'Um.'

Kulika smiled to herself and pushed away from the wall, stalking across the training ground towards her. 'It's easier if you try it in action, sometimes,' she said. 'Have you tried sparring yet?'

'No.' Quick didn't want to admit that she was such a pariah in the block that no one would partner with her.

'Do you want to?' Kulika asked, looking at Quick with a wicked glint in her eye.

Quick swallowed. Her mouth was suddenly dry. Now that Kulika was closer, all Quick could smell was the salty scent of her skin. She wanted to lean in and sniff it, but she held herself back, because that would probably be weird.

Correction: it would *definitely* be weird.

Kulika came to a stop just a step away from Quick. She was smiling.

'Well?' she prompted.

It felt like a dangerous proposal. Not only was Kulika

apparently a dangerous person, but Quick's reaction to her was dangerous as well. Quick had seen Kulika side by side with Bartholomew, so she knew just how involved she was with this place, but she still wanted Kulika with a fierceness that scared her. If she actually *touched* her again, even if they were fighting, Quick wasn't sure what would happen.

But she *really* wanted to find out.

Kulika had only been away from her gym in Oxford for a few days, but it felt like longer, to her mind and to her body. Having the chance to stretch out the kinks would have been welcome in any circumstances, but when Quick was her opponent, when every kick and punch she blocked would bring them thudding into contact with a joyful burst of uncontrolled impact?

From the first hit, she loved it so much that she already knew she'd never want to stop.

'I'm no good at this,' Quick said after her first swing.

Kulika had asked her to aim a punch at her face, and she'd thrown herself off balance and ended up falling into Kulika's arms. Her ready, waiting arms. It had been all Kulika could do to let Quick go after she'd put her back on her feet.

'Try again,' Kulika said, 'but this time, plant your feet a little wider, like this.'

Kulika demonstrated, and Quick imitated the stance perfectly. That was a good sign, but Kulika would have been lying if she'd said that a part of her hadn't been hoping Quick would need some adjustment. Her fingers were itching to touch her.

But no. She didn't want to force this. She would initiate contact only when strictly necessary for teaching purposes. Or when invited. God, she wished she would be invited. Quick hadn't tied up her hair, so it flowed loosely around her shoulders in a waterfall that Kulika longed to stroke. She wanted to run her fingers through it and see how it moved in the moonlight, how the colour changed when the light hit it at different angles. It was… distracting.

'Like this?' Quick asked, snapping Kulika's attention back to her stance.

'Right,' she said, clearing her throat. Why was her mouth suddenly so dry? 'Just raise your hands a little more. You're trying to guard your face.'

Quick lifted her arms in a way that pressed her cleavage together, drawing Kulika's gaze inexorably downwards.

'Better?' Quick asked.

When Kulika's attention snapped back this time, she found Quick looking at her with amusement. Seeing her smile, Kulika couldn't help but smile back. That was when Quick swung again, trying to take advantage of Kulika's distraction, which just made Kulika smile more.

This girl was *ruthless*.

And Kulika loved it.

Quick was eighty-five percent certain that Kulika had just been checking her out. Granted, this T-shirt scooped a little lower in the neck than Quick would have preferred, and when she raised her fists the effect it had on her body was eye-catching, but Quick was pretty sure she'd caught Kulika's eye in a good way.

Ninety percent certain.

It still wasn't enough, though. In the circumstances, she would have to be absolutely one hundred percent sure that Kulika was into her before she made a move, because the circumstances were dire. Quick was at the very bottom of the pile, trying to escape this place and take her friends with her, and Kulika was standing next to the man who seemed to have power of life and death over them all.

No, she couldn't be too careful. Perhaps she had distracted Kulika for a moment – ninety-five percent certain, given the way Kulika was looking at her now – but Quick herself couldn't afford to be distracted.

However alluring the distraction might be.

'I'm not very good at any of this,' she said apologetically.

'Because you're trying to force it,' said Kulika. 'It's tensing you up through the shoulders, so you're holding yourself back instead of reacting naturally. You're Silver, now. You're built for this. You've got the potential for enormous speed; you just have to let it fly. Look,' she said, then she put her hands on Quick's shoulders and Quick forgot to breathe. She wished suddenly that she'd picked a top from the wardrobe that was more like Kulika's, so more of her skin could have been bared to the other woman's touch. But then it was distracting enough to be touched by her like this, through the shoulders of her T-shirt.

If Kulika wanted her to relax, this was absolutely not the way to go about it.

Quick was absolutely letting herself get distracted.

Fuck.

'Guard up,' Kulika yelled as Quick swung again.

She was getting the hang of it surprisingly fast. Satisfyingly fast. It sometimes happened like this, usually with no warning. Kulika'd had a suspicion, though. These days, most people went through their adult lives never even throwing a punch. They didn't know how to do it, or how it felt, and they'd certainly never dream of doing it in polite society anyway, so why learn? Which meant they never found out if they were any good at fighting. But Quick had a natural affinity for it.

After a few more bouts of fist-fighting, Kulika introduced her to some basic kicks, and that was when the rest of her power finally unlocked. One minute Kulika was blocking a jab, then Quick stuck out a leg and tripped her up, rolling Kulika onto the ground. She wouldn't have caught Kulika out under normal circumstances, but Quick had done the whole thing moving at Silver speed. Unfortunately, she appeared to have caught herself out with it too, overshooting so she pitched face-first onto the ground.

On top of Kulika.

'Um,' Quick said.

They were chin to chin, nose to nose, close enough to kiss, and Kulika was oh so willing.

For one brief, joyful second, their eyes locked and Kulika thought Quick might actually be about to close the meagre distance that remained between them, but then Quick scrambled back to her feet, muttering, 'Sorry,' and Kulika could only regret the missed opportunity.

'Don't be sorry,' Kulika replied, jumping to her feet. 'You're getting it. You just moved at Silver speed on that last kick.'

'I did?'

'Did you not realise?'

Quick looked puzzled for a moment, then frustrated, then she looked away. Kulika wished she knew what had just happened inside her head, but Quick was giving nothing away.

'You can do this,' Kulika promised her. 'Just reset, and come at me again.'

The next time Quick started punching, it was serious. Having tapped into her power once, she was brimming with it now. She sped impossibly fast into dodges, she leapt impossibly high into kicks, and she hit Kulika so hard that it was almost a fair fight.

Kulika felt like yelling with the joy of it. She thrilled to it. She was an instrument of muscle and force, and Quick wasn't holding back. She didn't need to – yet – but Kulika was surprised by her strength, given how recently she'd been turned. It wouldn't be long before Kulika wouldn't need to hold back either, and the thought of that was enough to bring a grin to her bleeding lips.

She was *so* strong.

'I'm not sure I can carry on much longer,' Quick panted eventually.

'You need blood,' Kulika said. 'Using the speed burns through it.'

'Then I guess I won't be using it much.'

Quick wandered back over to the building and sat down with her back against the wall, leaning her head back against it as she caught her breath. The silver mark was gone from her neck, Kulika noticed. Probably the one in the roots of her hair too, though the waves were cascading so abundantly over Quick's shoulders that it was impossible to tell for sure.

God, Kulika wanted to reach out and touch it. Instead, she sat herself down beside Quick and looked up to the stars, trying to calm her hungry eyes with the sight of anything else.

'We need to talk about Evita,' Kulika said into the darkness.

'Do you know where she is?' Quick asked, her voice full of hope.

'No,' she replied. 'I'm looking for her, though.'

'Why?' Quick asked suspiciously.

Dammit. She was clever too.

'To bring her back here,' Kulika said.

'To him? For Bartholomew?'

'For all of us. She's crew.'

'Right,' Quick scoffed. 'You say that as though you expect it to reassure me.'

'This won't be forever,' Kulika whispered, with more hope than truth.

'People keep saying that, too, but again: not reassuring. *Why* won't it be forever? Because we're all going to get out of here and go back to our lives, safe and sound, or because we're heading towards something that's going to kill us all? The way people are talking around the block, it sounds to me like none of us are making it out of here alive.'

'*We* will,' Kulika said, with conviction she didn't feel.

'And Evita?' Quick asked.

'Her too. I'll find her. I'm good at finding people.'

'But you don't know her, not like I do.'

'She doesn't know herself,' Kulika countered. 'She lost her memory when she got turned. She's been calling herself Jane Doe.'

Quick laughed.

'I've been speaking to everyone who knew her when she was here,' Kulika went on, 'learning what I can. Have you heard anything that might help?'

'They won't talk about her,' Quick said. 'Last time I said the name Jane around here, I got someone killed.'

'Well, they talked to me. Not that Bartholomew gave them much choice about it. Do you know who Brandon and Penny are?'

'Yes,' Quick said, then she made a face.

'You don't like them?'

'Penny's being friendly enough, but she's part of the reason I ended up in the blood cellar. Brandon too. I don't like either of them much,' Quick admitted.

'Well, apparently Evita – or Jane – did,' said Kulika. 'The

three of them went on a cruise to Jamaica together, and only two of them came back. I can't find anyone who saw her again after the cruise left the island.'

'So she's still there?'

'We'll see. I'm flying out tomorrow. Well, later today.'

Kulika had booked the tickets the moment she'd realised Bayly was a no-show at the Convocation. It had been dark, yes, but Kulika was sure that he hadn't been there. She'd known Bayly for hundreds of years. She would recognise the scent of his blood from literally a mile away, and it had been nowhere in that hall this evening.

Which meant trouble, particularly since Kulika had definitely seen Enzo. She'd spoken to him before coming to the block, and he'd sworn up and down that he had no idea where Bayly had gone. She could think of no good scenario that explained Bayly's absence, on a night when Bartholomew had insisted all crew members be present. *The full complement*, he'd said, but he'd got at least one less than that. Two, if you counted Evita.

Maybe Kulika was worrying unnecessarily, but her gut told her that she'd find their two missing crew members together.

13

JANE DOE.

That was just like Evita, with her dark sense of humour. The familiarity of it made Quick's chest ache.

'I'm flying out tomorrow,' Kulika had said, which meant that she was allowed to leave the property, unlike Quick. She'd had to get special dispensation from Monty just to use the training ground.

It reminded Quick how little she knew about the woman sitting next to her in the dark, and how little she should trust her.

'I'm not sure I should even believe you,' Quick said quietly.

'About what?'

'About finding Evita, about getting out of here. About anything. I don't know you.'

'I suppose not,' Kulika replied quietly.

'But I *want* to trust you. So who are you?' Quick asked.

An awkward expression flitted across Kulika's face. 'I'm Kulika Yadav,' she said.

'Yes, I know,' Quick replied impatiently. 'But who *are* you? You said you were going to help us escape the cellar, but then you were standing next to Bartholomew at the Casting and again at the Convocation. He called you his Second. They say that makes you… Well, put it this way, if they knew you were here with me right now I'm pretty sure they'd bump me up the board by about a hundred points.'

'The board?'

'Forget it. The point is, you made me into *this*, then you saved me yesterday and suddenly you're training me… But the others act like they're scared of you, and it sounds like that's with good reason, and I don't understand how you can be that and this at the same time. You said you were part of Bartholomew's crew. *Were*, past tense, but it doesn't look like that from where I'm sitting, and I don't understand any of it.'

'What are you asking me?' Kulika's expression was almost offended, and Quick didn't understand that, either.

'I just want to know where you stand. Where *I* stand.'

Kulika pushed her hair away from her face in a gesture that looked to Quick like she was buying time.

'You kissed me,' Quick said. 'And it was—'

'It takes away the pain,' Kulika explained quickly. 'If I hadn't, it would have hurt when I bit you.'

Quick's mouth went dry. The way Kulika described the kiss, it was as though she'd just injected Quick with a little anaesthetic, but the effect of it on Quick had been far from numbing. She hadn't trusted her feelings at the time, barely daring to believe that Kulika might actually want her. From the way Kulika was talking now, it seemed Quick was right to have been cautious. She hadn't been cautious enough, though, because the realisation that the kiss had been merely practical – the last thing a kiss should ever be – crushed Quick's fragile psyche into a paste on the dirt.

Stupid, she thought.

Then she cleared her throat and said, 'I see,' because she'd been sitting in silence for a while now and she had to say *something*. 'And what about being Bartholomew's Second?'

'What about it?' Kulika was getting defensive now, in a way that twisted something in Quick's stomach. She didn't want to think about what might be causing that defensiveness, but at the same time, she had to know. If this was it, if Kulika and Bartholomew were involved, then she'd rather know now so she could put to rest whatever feelings were still trying to sprout their way out of the broken mess of her heart.

She only had herself to blame. There was a very good reason that she only did flings and never relationships: all her life people had abandoned her, starting with her parents, so she'd learned to be careful with her feelings. In fact, she'd become so good at protecting them over the years that pushing people away had become more instinct than choice.

But Kulika was somehow different. Without even meaning to, Quick had started to let her in. On the night of the Casting, Quick had reminded herself of all the reasons that Kulika didn't actually want her. It made perfect sense from a practical standpoint: Kulika was a vampire, and she'd wanted Quick's blood. Now Quick knew there was a further layer of practicality: Kulika had kissed her so the bite wouldn't hurt, so she wouldn't make a fuss about it. Now that Quick had further context for how the Silver in this place worked and the twisted games they played with each other for status, it was clear that Kulika had a practical reason for turning Quick Silver, too: it would bump *her* up the hierarchy. If her recent promotion to Bartholomew's Second was any indication, that ploy had been very successful indeed.

But none of that explained why Kulika was here now,

sitting in the dirt with Quick. Could Quick really have imagined the tension between them as they sparred? Had it truly only been her who'd felt the press of their bodies together in the scrum and wished they could be closer still?

'Why are you here, Kulika?' Quick asked, a simple question to stop the rest of her thoughts from spilling out.

'I don't...' Kulika was drawing patterns in the dirt with her fingers. Evasive. 'It's complicated.'

'Then tell me something that isn't,' Quick said desperately. 'But tell me *something*. Tell me where you're from, what your favourite colour is, how old you are.'

'I've been Silver since 1721.' Kulika said the date so casually that it took Quick a while to process the fact that she'd said *seventeen* twenty-one instead of *twenty* twenty-one. It shouldn't have been a surprise, given the brief details Kulika had already let slip, but it knocked the wind right out of Quick's chest.

'1721?' she parroted back.

'Bartholomew turned me,' she said, looking down at her hands as they drew in the dirt, away towards the horizon, then back at the dirt. She never looked at Quick. 'I'm the only person he's ever turned. He cares about that.'

'So you're...' Quick scrambled for a way to phrase things delicately, while a stone settled heavily in her stomach. 'You and Bartholomew, you're a couple?'

'No,' Kulika said immediately, looking at Quick now. 'God, no. Never.'

Which stamped down the last shreds of hope that Quick had been harbouring for her and Kulika. The way Monty had talked about it before the Casting, she'd come to believe that turning someone Silver was kind of... sexy. It had certainly *felt* sexy, and Monty'd said you had to feel something for the person you turned, or vice versa, and then there'd been the kiss, so had she really been so wrong to assume that Kulika might have felt about her the way that Quick had begun to feel about Kulika?

But if there had been nothing between Kulika and the person who'd turned her Silver…

God, no.

It all made Quick feel naïve and ashamed.

'We were never involved,' Kulika added. 'I guess you could say I was Bartholomew's Second back then, too, as I am again now.'

'You support what he's doing here?' Quick asked, trying not to let the pain creep into her tone. She didn't want to believe that Kulika was on board with everything that had happened to Quick in this place, and to her and Xiaoyu in the cellar, and with everything Bartholomew was planning to do. She didn't want to believe that Kulika really was one of *them*.

'I didn't say that,' Kulika replied.

'But you're not going to stop him, either.'

'It's complicated,' Kulika said again, looking frustrated now.

'It looks pretty simple from where I'm sitting.'

'Is it?' Kulika asked, looking into Quick's eyes. 'Really? Why are you here, then, if you don't want to be part of his crew?'

'I need to find Evita.'

'I told you: I'm working on that.'

'And get Xiaoyu and the others out of here.'

'Then go open the cellar. I'll run interference while you free them,' Kulika said, with every indication that she was absolutely serious.

'But… I can't just…' Quick sat and scrambled for a moment before saying, 'I need an actual *plan* first. I signed the covenant, apparently. The others would find me and kill me before I got out of the county.'

'Right,' Kulika said. 'So maybe we're both stuck doing bad things for good reasons.'

Quick didn't know what to say to that, but apparently they were arguing now. Kulika's expression had become stern, her jaw set and her brow furrowed. She was looking up at the stars as though she bore them a grudge.

'You should get some rest,' Kulika said after a minute or so of silence. 'Refuel with blood.'

'Rest, yes. Blood, no. I'm not allowed,' Quick said. Kulika still looked bewildered, so Quick explained the points system and the board. 'I have to earn it,' Quick finished, 'and I'm failing miserably at that.'

'Then I'll get them to give you some blood.'

'Don't bother,' Quick said. 'They'll only dock me even more points that I don't have. I can manage on my own.'

'You don't have to.'

'No,' Quick said, feeling more convinced of it than ever. 'I think I do, actually. That's how things work here. But you *could* show me where the blood cellar is,' she added grudgingly. 'I can't remember the way.'

Kulika obliged, silently leading Quick through the ground floor of the block to a hidden cupboard set into the wall. No wonder she hadn't been able to find it by herself; she'd been looking in the right area, but unless you knew exactly where to look, it seemed like just an ordinary stretch of wall.

'How did you know it was there?' Quick asked Kulika.

Kulika tapped the side of her nose and said, 'Silver senses improve as you age.'

'And you're three hundred years old,' Quick remembered. 'Right.'

It was a hell of an age gap, just one of the many reasons

that pining after Kulika was a terrible idea.

'Well, thanks,' Quick said. 'I guess I'll go to bed now.' That was a lie, obviously. She fully intended to crack open the hatch the moment Kulika left so she could check Xiaoyu was all right. Then she could make some kind of a plan to come back here later when she knew she wouldn't be interrupted.

'He won't let you take them,' Kulika said quietly.

'Excuse me?'

'You might be able to break into the place and snatch some blood if you're quick, but you'll never get more than a few seconds before they realise what you're doing and stop you.'

'Why? Are you going to tell them?' Quick asked, revving up to get angry.

Kulika didn't match her energy. Instead, she said, 'No, but Bartholomew knows everything that happens on his property. He's watching me, so he'll be watching you.'

'Cameras?' Quick looked up into the corners of the corridor ceiling. She should have thought of it earlier.

But Kulika just tapped her nose again and said, 'Silver senses. They're stronger than you seem to realise.'

'Strong enough for you to know what's going on down there without opening the hatch?' Quick asked, as an idea occurred to her.

Kulika raised an eyebrow, and Quick took it as an invitation.

'I drank from Xiaoyu, and she was already weak, but they took her away before I could check she was okay, and now I'm worried I might have killed her,' Quick said, the words rushing out like water. 'Can you...? Do you think you could just...?'

'The cellar's soundproofed,' Kulika said. 'Sorry.'

'Makes sense,' Quick replied. 'I guess Bartholomew didn't want the Silver in the dorms to be disturbed by the noise.'

Kulika's expression changed, then. 'How bad was it down there?'

'Bad.'

Quick didn't want to elaborate. She didn't want to remember the zombie, and the broken bones when the new humans were chucked in, and the terror in the dark when she hadn't known what was coming down through the hatch next. Most of all, she didn't want to think about the fact that she was now part of the reason the blood cellar existed. She had to get her blood from somewhere, however rarely she was allowed it, and it was coming from down there.

'Night, then,' Quick said abruptly.

'Oh,' Kulika said, looking like she wanted to talk more, but she still said, 'Night.'

Quick smiled a tight smile and walked away down the corridor towards the stairs that led to the dorm. With every step, she felt the urge to turn back and repair things with Kulika, or just throw herself into her arms and kiss her, but all of those urges were proposed by her body and vetoed by her brain.

She needed to be on her own. She needed to think, and she couldn't do that around Kulika, surrounded by so much uncertainty and mistrust. Part of Quick wanted so much to open up to her, but the part of her that had kept her alive this long was begging her to count up the red flags and run in the opposite direction.

Belatedly, that's exactly what she did.

She couldn't trust Kulika, or anyone else in this place. The only people she could ever trust were herself and Evita. Maybe she'd revise that opinion if Kulika came up trumps and actually did find her friend, but if not, then Quick would get out of here and do it herself.

Not without Xiaoyu and the others, though.

If Bartholomew's senses were strong enough to surveil the block from the house, then that was a serious spanner in the works. But just because he had the ability to point his senses out here, that didn't mean he *would* if his attention was directed elsewhere. Which meant the only way Quick had any hope of getting into the cellar was to create the kind of distraction he wouldn't be able to ignore.

Maybe it was time to take a cue from the Silver further up the board, and start setting shit on fire.

14

AFTER SUNDAY NIGHT'S party, which continued until well after dawn on Monday, none of the higher-ranking Silver were awake to crack the whip. Most of them were lying around unconscious in the big common room, spilling through the glass doors out onto the deck by the training ground, and generally making a mess of themselves.

But not all of them were asleep when Quick ventured downstairs from the dorm, which was going to throw a spanner in her quest for fire-lighting materials.

'It's too fucking crowded in here,' Bella was complaining, kicking an unconscious Silver off the sofa by the deck so she could sit down.

When that Silver landed on the floor, he groaned and rolled over to look up at Bella. It was Brandon.

'Then find us somewhere bigger,' he shot back at her sleepily. 'You were supposed to be looking.'

'I have been. Everywhere's too small and shitty and there's not enough space to build.'

'Then look harder. Christ, Bella. Anyone would think you wanted to stay here forever.'

'Just shut up, will you?' Monty said. Quick hadn't noticed

him immediately, but she recognised his voice and followed it to an armchair facing the deck, where he sat rubbing at his temples. 'I'm trying to think.'

'And I'm trying to find a suitable headquarters for a hostile takeover of the whole fucking world,' said Bella. 'What makes you think your job's more important than mine?'

'The fact that it fucking is!' Monty snapped. 'You're window dressing. I'm doing the actual work. Just get the hell out of here and go find a place with a big enough pool house or whatever bullshit thing will make you happy. I'm trying to build a dynasty, here.'

'With your one little successful Silver disciple?' Bella said mockingly. 'Angelina's not much of a dynasty.'

'With Bartholomew's whole fucking army!'

'Will you both shut up?' Brandon groaned.

He wasn't the only one who was disturbed by their argument, if the moans coming from around the room were any indication.

'Some army this is,' Bella said, turning to survey the partied-out Silver who were filling the floor. In the process, she caught sight of Quick hesitating in the doorway. Her eyes narrowed. 'Oh, look,' she said to Monty. 'Here's one of your many failures now.'

Monty glanced up, saw it was Quick, and replied, 'Not exactly a failure when she got me on the top of the board, is she?'

'Because of Kulika Yadav,' Bella argued, 'not because of you.'

'I'm the one who brought her here, aren't I?'

'And dumped her just as quickly.'

'Like Enzo dumped you, you mean?' Monty said acidly.

'He didn't dump me,' Bella replied. 'He's back, isn't he?

He came back for me.'

'Sure about that, are you? Where did he sleep last night?'

Bella went still for a moment, her eyes narrowing further as she glared at Monty, then she snapped out of it abruptly, crossed the room towards Quick, grabbed her arm and said, 'Come on, Failure. We're going house-hunting.'

'She hasn't earned the points to go off-base,' Monty said.

'Well, does anyone else want to come with me?' Unsurprisingly, there were no volunteers. 'That's what I thought. Maybe this way she can actually start earning her way up the board.'

'Okay,' Monty said speculatively. 'Two-fifty for you if you find us a place. A hundred for Quick if she helps.'

'Three hundred for me,' Bella countered.

'Fine. Now get out of here.'

'Gladly,' Bella said, exiting the room backwards with a mocking bow, dragging Quick along beside her. When they were halfway down the corridor, she muttered, 'Prick.'

'Yeah, he is,' Quick agreed.

'I wasn't talking to you,' said Bella. 'Go shower and find something classy but sexy in the wardrobe. Fast. Do your hair and make up too. You can't go house-hunting for multi-million dollar properties in sweats, looking like someone pulled you out of bed through a hurricane.'

Quick did as she was told, doing her best with the tools she had to work with, which were a limited selection of clothing and a make up bag she found in the wardrobe containing products that did not suit her colouring at all. She tried, but she had to smother on the sunscreen if they were going outside to avoid going up in flames, and it didn't play well with the make up. Bella was quicker with her own transformation, shedding her slept-in party dress for a classily understated skirt and jacket combo that showed off her curves to their best advantage. When she saw Quick with her pink dress and black parasol, she sighed.

'New plan,' Bella said. 'Find a plain suit and wipe off the clown make up. You can be my chauffeur.'

Quick went back into the wardrobe, and came out again having made the required changes. The skirt suit was a little snug around the waist, and she couldn't button the jacket, but if she was staying in the car then it would do.

'Acceptable,' Bella confirmed, looking her up and down. 'You need sunglasses to hide the silver in your eyes, though,' she added, sending Quick back into the wardrobe to find a pair. When she emerged once more, Bella said, 'You drive, right?'

'Yes.'

'Automatic or stick?'

'Manual transmission,' Quick said. 'Stick, I guess.'

'That's not what I've heard,' Bella said, then she laughed like this was the funniest joke she'd ever heard.

It wound Quick up enough to make her reckless. 'Who's Enzo?' she asked.

Oh, she should not have asked that question. For a moment, Bella looked angry to the point of going feral, but she pinned her lips shut and instead gestured sharply for Quick to follow her out of the block, into the muggy morning heat, and over to the mansion.

Where they found a man standing on the porch, drinking coffee. He was freshly-showered and stylishly-dressed in chinos and an ironed shirt. Everything about him looked expensive. Even from across the lawn, Quick had a suspicion he would smell amazing.

Seeing him, Bella's entire demeanour changed. The tension went out of her shoulders, the fierce grimace disappeared from her face, and her entire body inclined towards him like a sunflower bending towards the sun.

'Enzo,' Bella called to him softly.

When he looked their way and saw Bella approaching, his eyes widened a little and he moved back from the rail, almost as if he was scared of her. That did not bode well.

'Were you waiting for me to wake up?' she cooed at him in a tone more saccharine than Quick had ever heard her use before. 'God, I was starting to think you'd abandoned me here forever. When you said you were coming back, I thought you meant in maybe a week, not in *six months*.' She laughed, a sound of pure relieved joy, but stopped abruptly when she realised that Enzo wasn't smiling back at her. 'What's happened?' she asked solicitously.

'I'm…' He looked over his shoulder into the house, then back at Bella. 'I can't talk right now.'

'Enzo.' Bella smiled at him in incomprehension. 'What do you mean, you can't talk? You haven't seen me in half a year. You could at least say hello. Can't you?'

But he was looking back over his shoulder again. 'I—'

'You came back for me, right?' Bella said, getting angry now as she strode towards the porch. 'You had to be away to finish your mission for Bartholomew, but it's over now, and you came back for *me*, because you love me. Don't you?' There were angry tears in her eyes.

Quick didn't know what to do. It felt wrong to be standing here witnessing what was clearly a lovers' tiff, but she also didn't feel like she could just go off on her own unsupervised, so instead she stood by the edge of the pool like a lemon with her parasol, looking at her feet and trying not to feel Bella's pain.

That was when Bartholomew sauntered out onto the porch, his eyes directed down at the phone in his hands as he went to join Enzo.

'My Second is on her way to Jamaica,' he said without looking up, 'searching for your boyfriend. You'd better hope she can find him, because if she doesn't then it's bad news for you.'

'Boyfriend?' Bella asked in a small voice.

'Oh.' Bartholomew finally looked up. 'I didn't realise we had company.' That was surely a lie. If his senses were as powerful as Kulika had led Quick to believe they were, he would have known they were headed this way the moment they left the block.

'Boyfriend?' Bella asked again, turning a wave of wrath on Enzo. 'You have a *boyfriend*?'

'He does,' Bartholomew said with a blithe smile. 'Bayly. How long has it been now, Enzo? About seven or eight months?'

'About that,' Enzo said quietly.

'*Bayly*?' Bella screeched.

But Bartholomew was already heading back into the house, calling Enzo along behind him like a dog. He went running, leaving Bella to gape after him.

For a few long seconds, she didn't move.

'Are you okay?' Quick said.

For a few more seconds, Bella still didn't move, then she turned sharply and strode off around the side of the house. Quick had to run to keep up. When Bella reached the driveway, she walked to the mansion's front door, slammed her way through it and into a small utility area behind it, then started rifling through a rack of car keys until she found the one she wanted. Just as Quick had managed to scramble into the room behind her, she turned and slammed her way back out again, letting the door close in Quick's face. Quick scrambled back outside again, chasing hurricane Bella.

'Fuck him,' Bella muttered as she crossed the drive. 'I've

been waiting in this shithole for six months. *Six months*. He said he loved me, you know. They always *say* they love you, but that's just because you have something they want, isn't it? And I had the keys to the lab. I thought, when I let him do this to me,' she said, gesturing at her silver-threaded eyes, 'I thought, hey, a whole lifetime together sounds fun. *Romantic*. I was a fucking fool,' she spat. 'He was fucking that grumpy old pirate the whole time.' Bella laughed then, the kind of laughter that might so easily have tipped into tears.

That was when Quick started to worry, because it was clear that none of this was directed at her. In fact, it was as though Bella had forgotten Quick was there.

Quick followed Bella to the car that matched the keys Bella had selected, an unnecessarily large SUV that was so high it would challenge the stretch fabric of Quick's skirt to get into the damn thing. Bella was headed for the driver's seat until Quick said, 'Didn't you want me to drive?'

Then Bella blinked and turned back towards Quick, looking at her as though she'd just appeared from nowhere.

'Chauffeur,' she said.

'Right,' said Quick.

'Yes,' Bella agreed, then she tossed Quick the keys and circled the car to hop into the passenger side, muttering to herself the whole way. 'Into Charleston, then, to the first realtor's office,' she said distractedly. 'I'll tell you where to turn.'

Quick hopped into the driver's sear, closing the parasol only after she was in the safety of the filter glass, then she put the car into gear and rolled it down the drive. She had a suspicion this outing was going to be more trouble than it was worth, even for a hundred points. Even for a thousand points. But she was committed now, and she didn't have much choice but to see it through.

15

WALKING AWAY FROM Quick the night before had been one of the hardest things Kulika had ever had to do. It was clear that Quick didn't trust her, and no wonder. They'd only known each other a few days, and during those few days they'd only met on a handful of occasions. On half of those occasions Kulika had ended up biting someone, and on half of *those* occasions the person she'd bitten had been Quick. Really, they weren't the kind of statistics that inspired trust.

Kulika had no such qualms about Quick. She loved her, from the top of her sunset hair to the bottom of her dirt-caked toes. Whatever happened at the mansion while she was away, whatever Quick did, *who*ever she turned out to be once Kulika had a chance to get to know her, it would make no difference. Kulika was in it for the long haul, regardless. Quick would be her person from now until the day one of them died. Either way, Kulika wouldn't survive Quick.

She was in exactly the same situation as Baron Drake now, and look where that had landed him. If she couldn't find Evita Khalyed and get Dr Ross to make this antidote, then Jack would die, so the baron would die, creating a power vacuum she was sure Bartholomew would be only too happy to fill.

Kulika meditated on that as she drove to the airport and caught her plane to Jamaica. It didn't take more than five minutes of flight time for her to realise that, even if she was Bartholomew's Second, allowing him to achieve world domination wouldn't be good for any of them. That knowledge made her a restless traveller, fidgeting in her seat all the way to Kingston. She needed to find Dr Khalyed, and she needed to find her now, but she couldn't run over water, so here she was stuck in a metal box in the sky, painfully aware that by the time she arrived Bayly would have had a least a day's head start.

Longer than that, as it turned out. The plane landed in the early afternoon, but it took Kulika until long after dark to track Bayly's scent to the right spot. She'd assumed he'd be somewhere in Port Royal, maybe even in old Port Royal itself, off the edge of the current harbour line, digging around in the remains of the sunken city. Instead, she finally ran Bayly's scent to ground in the old graveyard on the Palisadoes, a thin stretch of land that was now little more than rocky, scrubby sand to either side of the highway, a meagre bulwark between the road and the sea.

She should have come here first. She alone of all the crew suspected what Bayly had buried here in the earthquake of 1692. Or, rather, *whom*. He'd told her once, and only once, when he was sunk deep into a bottle. The mention was so brief that she hadn't been sure he meant what he was saying, or how seriously she should take him. Just six horrific little words: *Buried Digs alive with old Morgan.*

Digs, she knew, had been his lover once, the man who turned him Silver. And Morgan... Well, every pirate worth their salt knew who Henry Morgan was. But Bayly had never mentioned it again, and Kulika knew enough not to go digging up other people's buried treasure.

Evita Khalyed hadn't been Bayly's to bury in the first place, though. The Silver could technically live forever locked away like that, without light or air or blood, just withering slowly into dust and madness. But Khalyed was new, and Kulika had no idea exactly how long she'd been underground. A month? Two months? She could only hope that she wasn't too late.

Bayly was nowhere to be seen, but his scent dead-ended at the water's edge and pooled there, as though he'd lingered for some time. She found the exact spot easily enough. It had been disturbed recently and cleared of scrub, so the sand and rocks sat awkwardly amongst each other with only a few uprooted weeds for company. Kulika started digging.

She wasn't alone for long.

'Kulika,' he said, stopping in the surf.

'Bayly.'

'You worked it out, then.'

'Eventually,' she said, getting to her feet. 'I heard a couple of the kids decided to take a cruise out here and I thought to myself, *why Jamaica, of all places*?'

Bayly shrugged. 'It's a nice place.'

'It's a hot, sticky place in high summer, and they were already in a hot, sticky place with its own blood bank. No, I don't think they came here on holiday. Then I thought, I know someone who likes to spend time on this island in particular, because he's got history here, and it turns out that you went on a little holiday of your own around the same time that Brandon and Penny and "Jane" took theirs.'

'They told you about the treasure, then.'

'Neither Brandon nor Penny is very good at keeping a secret, and they're more scared of me than they are of you.'

'With good reason. They've heard enough about you.

Bartholomew tells them,' Bayly said. 'Bedtime stories for the crew. Something to give them nightmares.'

'Where's Evita?' Kulika asked.

Bayly said nothing, but he was edging slowly up the beach and around to one side as he spoke, trying to put the land at his back instead of the sea. This would end in a fight, then. It would be a fight that Bayly would lose. He'd never had the upper hand on Kulika, and she wasn't about to let him get it now. He didn't have her edge, or the anger she used to sharpen it.

'You buried her here with Digs, didn't you?' Kulika asked.

She could tell from the look on his face that she'd guessed right.

'You could have told me where she was whenever you liked,' Kulika growled. 'You knew, Bayly, all along. You knew what it meant to me, going back to that mansion. You knew that the moment I walked through that door I'd be surrendering my life, my freedom, everything I've worked so hard to build over the past hundred years, and *still* you said nothing. We were right there,' she said, pointing back towards Port Royal. 'You sat on that harbour wall with me before I'd even set foot back on the mainland. You knew full well where I was going, and why, and still you let me go. You let me go, knowing all the time that the person I was looking for was buried right here, not even two miles away from where we sat.' Kulika's fists clenched at her sides, her fingertips digging into her palms.

'You're too late, anyway,' Bayly said quietly, edging further around. 'I moved her.'

'No,' Kulika said as cold washed over her skin.

'I knew you'd work it out sooner or later. You're not stupid, but then neither am I.'

His back was almost to the highway now, and Kulika's

was almost to the sea, but she couldn't bring herself to care. It didn't matter where he manoeuvred himself. She'd fight him underwater if she had to, but one way or another she would make him pay for delivering her back into Bartholomew's hands.

She wasn't sure who moved first. Probably her, but with Silver speed and Silver reactions, there wasn't much to choose between a fraction of a second here or there. They crashed together in the centre just the same, punching and head-butting and brawling in the dirtiest of dirty fights. Kulika got her knee in Bayly's crotch, and he got his fist wrapped around her hair, and after that it was a melée of teeth and nails that ended with both of them broken and only half-healed, but Kulika on top with her fingertips digging into Bayly's throat.

'You've only got yourself to blame for this,' she said, spitting blood. 'You're the one who let him get me on a chain again.'

'I only let you fall in love, same as me,' he gasped out through gritted teeth.

'I'm *crew*!' she yelled into his reddening face. 'You were supposed to look out for me!'

'You *were* crew!' he yelled back. 'You're not anymore!'

'I *am*!' Kulika yelled one last time, then she abruptly released her grip and fell back on the rocky sand, staring at the man who had once been – and was, she realised, once more – her crewmate. 'I am, Bayly,' she said quietly. 'I'm crew. Again.'

He looked at her hopelessly, and she looked hopelessly back, one caged animal to another. At that, their fight was over, as quickly as it had begun.

'Where is she?' Kulika asked eventually, wiping the blood from her mouth.

Bayly just looked at her through helpless eyes. He wouldn't tell her.

'Will you at least tell me why?' Kulika asked.

'For Enzo,' Bayly replied.

'*For* Enzo? Does Khalyed mean something to him?'

'She means freedom,' he replied simply, but he wouldn't elaborate. He just shook his head and fell silent.

'You know you've broken the covenant,' Kulika said. 'You know Bartholomew won't let it slide.'

'Article two,' Bayly murmured.

'At least. *If any man rob another he shall have his nose and ears slit, and be put ashore where he shall be sure to encounter hardships.*'

'We're already ashore, Kulika, and I've encountered hardships enough.'

Hadn't they all?

That was when it had all started to go wrong, on the day Bartholomew had sold his ships to buy the mansion. It had put them so tantalisingly close to the sea, and yet a whole world away. None of them had wanted to settle down, but the British had been cracking down on piracy, and there was no way to be subtle about a crew as large as Bartholomew's, or to muscle their way through. Bartholomew and a few of the others might have had the strength, but the rest were only human, and turning them Silver en masse hadn't been an option. Without the formula that had just been developed by BioSilver, their odds would have been about one in a hundred for each attempt, and that was with generous estimates. Three hundred years ago, turning people Silver just hadn't been that simple.

Kulika supposed she should be grateful for Bartholomew's success with her.

'The old punishments don't hold, anyway,' Bayly said

with resignation. 'You know that. With the new Articles, it's death every time.'

'I'll still have to take you in.'

'He'll kill Enzo,' Bayly said, looking at Kulika with pleading eyes. 'I'm too old and too hardened for him to bump me off any other way. He'll kill us both.'

'And if I don't bring you in, what do you think he'll do to Quick when he finds out?'

Bayly licked his lips nervously. 'Maybe he doesn't have to find out.'

Kulika gave Bayly a dubious look, because really? He knew as well as she did that Bartholomew would *always* find out, then he'd make them all pay for it.

'No, listen,' Bayly said quickly. 'What if you gave me a week? Just… give me a few days to get my business straight. The crew can wait that long to get her back, can't they?'

'Baron Drake can't,' Kulika replied flatly. 'He needs her blood so the doctor can make his antidote, and he needs it now.'

'Blood I can do,' Bayly said excitedly, as though Kulika had already agreed. 'Look, I'll get Jane's blood and bring it to you. You can give it to your doctor. Hell, I'll even ask Enzo to lend her his lab space so she can work.'

'Bartholomew'll find out.'

'He won't,' Bayly insisted. 'How could he? Just—'

'He will find out.'

'How, unless you're going to tell him? Or are you all in on this plan of his? You back to following Captain Roberts, pretending like he gives a shit about any of us?'

Kulika nearly went back to punching him. 'Of course he doesn't give a shit!' she yelled, throwing a handful of rocks at her crewmate. 'Jesus, Bayly. You really think I'm buying it?'

'I think it looks a lot like that lately.'

Which touched a nerve with Kulika, maybe because she knew he wasn't entirely wrong. 'Well, it isn't,' she insisted. 'I know him, better than even you do. He's not doing any of this for us. He just wants to have the world fit his idea of what it should be. He sees imperfection in everything around him, and because it can't be exactly the way he wants it to be, he wants to burn it up and start again. Assuming, of course, that he'll survive the burning. The annoying thing is,' she said, tossing a stone at the road, 'he's probably right.'

'Then give me a little grace, would you?'

She shook her head. 'It's too risky.'

'Please, Kulika. I'm begging you. One day.'

'I can't just—'

'I'd do it for you if it was Quick on the line.'

Kulika shouldn't have hesitated. She should have dragged Bayly back to Bartholomew, kicking and screaming if necessary. She should have dragged Enzo out of his rooms, then threatened him until Bayly gave up Evita Khalyed's location. It's what the old pirate Kulika would have done. It's what the baron's bodyguard would have done too, just a week ago, knowing that the baron's life was on the line.

But it was Bayly, and he was in exactly the same situation with Enzo that she found herself in with Quick. She softened, and he saw it.

She *softened*.

That wasn't like her at all.

'I'll get the blood,' Bayly said quickly, already backing away to the road. 'Just meet me in Waterfront Park, down on the pier. Midday. I'll bring it to you.'

Then he was gone, disappearing in a blur of Silver speed. She could have followed, she supposed. Probably should have done, but she'd burned a lot of energy today searching for him, it had been too long since she'd last drunk any blood, and she wasn't ready to put on the speed.

She'd have to get a flight back to Charleston, and even then she'd barely make it back in time to meet Bayly the next day. Doubtless that was exactly as he'd planned it. He always had been more cunning than he looked.

Kulika sighed and pulled her phone out of her pocket. It was the middle of the night in the UK, the early hours of Tuesday morning, but he picked up on the third ring.

'Send Dr Ross,' she said without preamble.

'You've found her?'

'Not exactly,' Kulika replied, 'But I'll have her blood tomorrow.'

'Good enough,' the baron said.

Kulika hoped like hell that it would be, for all of their sakes.

16

KULIKA HADN'T INTENDED to ask Bartholomew's permission for Dr Ross to work in Enzo's lab at BioSilver. She hadn't intended to tell him anything at all, but circumstances conspired against her.

Dr Ross arrived earlier than expected the next morning, while Kulika was still making her way back to the mansion, somehow managing to fly across the Atlantic in less than the time it had taken Kulika to hop back to Charleston from Jamaica. If Kulika'd had her way, Dr Ross would never have set foot on Bartholomew's property, but clearly Baron Drake hadn't briefed the doctor about how dangerous his rival could be – or at least, not sufficiently – because she was sitting in the library drinking tea with the man himself when Kulika returned.

'Ah,' Bartholomew said as Kulika rushed into the library, anxiously following Dr Ross's scent to the very heart of the mansion. 'You know my Second, I think?' he said to the doctor.

'Your Sec— Kulika?' Dr Ross said, looking between the two of them, bewildered.

She hadn't known, of course. Kulika hadn't told the baron

about her recent promotion when she'd spoken to him on the phone, for obvious reasons. If she was supposed to be anyone's Second, it was his, not Bartholomew's. There'd be no stopping that particular piece of treachery from spreading now. When Tabitha Ross went back to the UK – *if* Bartholomew let her go back to the UK – she'd take with her the news that Kulika had defected. It had been inevitable that Baron Drake would find out sooner or later. If Kulika was lucky, maybe she could persuade Dr Ross to give her time to call him so she could break the news to him herself. She owed him that, at least.

'I wasn't expecting you so soon, Dr Ross,' Kulika said, lingering in the doorway. 'I would have met you at the airport if I'd known when your plane was getting in.'

'Oh well,' the doctor said, forcing a smile. 'No harm done. I'm here now.'

The doctor was a small, round woman dressed in a colourful skirt and T-shirt. She had a mess of long brown curls that she kept pinned up in a bun using whatever utensils came to hand – today it was a coffee stirrer and a disposable toothbrush that she'd probably got on the plane. Her face was round and expressive, which made it difficult for her to hide her discomfort. Dr Ross clearly didn't want to be in this room any more than Kulika wanted her here.

'Did you find Bayly and the girl?' Bartholomew asked Kulika.

'Not yet,' she said. 'But I know where he'll be at midday.'

'Then go and bring him in. I can look after the doctor.'

'Actually, sir…' Kulika was trying to be deferential, to get on Bartholomew's good side for the favour she was about to ask, but she could see from the look on his face that she'd already made a serious misstep. 'Primus,' she corrected herself, then she watched as Dr Ross attempted to control her shock. 'I thought perhaps Enzo could allow Dr Ross some lab space at BioSilver. Just for a day or so, for her work.'

'And what work is that, precisely?' Bartholomew asked.

Shit.

It had been arrogant of Kulika to think that she could play both sides and get away clean. Bartholomew was *always* watching.

'You told me I could complete my mission for Baron Drake.'

'But I didn't tell you that you could compromise Enzo's cover at BioSilver in the process. What exactly do you expect me to say to Solomon if he discovers that Dr Ross is working at his facility, in my territory, in the office of a man he believed to be a human research student?'

'That you know nothing,' Kulika suggested. 'Besides, Enzo already has everything you need from BioSilver. Doesn't he? Does it really matter if we burn him? It's just for a day or two.'

Bartholomew thought on this a while, then said, 'Fine. I'll let Enzo take Dr Ross to the lab, but you bring him and Bayly back here before the end of the day.'

'Yes, Primus. Thank you, Primus. If you're ready, doctor?'

Kulika ushered the doctor out of the library and through the mansion as quickly as she could.

Dr Ross started talking before they'd even reached the door, saying, 'What was that all—'

'Shh,' Kulika interrupted her quietly. 'Not here.'

Enzo was waiting on the porch, just where Kulika had expected to find him, wearing a linen suit and lounging like a catalogue model with a tiny espresso cup in his hand. Kulika had no idea where he'd got it from; the house didn't have a machine.

'Enzo!' she yelled at him. She'd hoped to startle him

enough to stain that fancy suit of his with coffee, but all she managed to do was burn his fingers. It was something, though.

'Kulika,' he said quickly. 'I didn't know what Bayly was doing. I promise, I didn't—'

'You can shut up right now,' she said. 'Get the keys to the truck and meet us out front.'

Enzo scuttled off through the house, leaving Kulika and Dr Ross alone on the deck. Dr Ross was carrying an old-fashioned doctor's bag, but nothing else. No suitcase, no other hand luggage. She obviously wasn't expecting to stay long.

'You've got the formula in there?' Kulika asked, nodding at the bag.

'In a little cooler, yes. I had a devil of a time getting it through customs, I can tell you. Baron Drake had to put in a call.'

There was an awkward silence, which Kulika broke by saying, 'I'm sorry I wasn't there to meet you.'

'It's okay,' Dr Ross said sadly, looking down at her patent plum flats.

'I would have been there if I could, but—'

'It's okay,' she said again. 'You've got a lot going on here, I can see.' The words sounded sympathetic, but her tone was snippy and judgemental.

'I have,' Kulika said. 'But it's not what you think.'

'I think Jack's going to die without this antidote, and you've chosen to spend your time manoeuvring yourself into a better position instead of trying to save her life.'

'It's not what you think,' Kulika said again.

The doctor ignored her, her expression set somewhere between sadness and extreme ire, so Kulika grabbed her by the hand and started leading her down the porch steps.

'I don't—'

'Just come with me,' Kulika insisted, so the doctor let herself be led past the pool, across the lawn, through the trees to the cleared space where the block stood. Kulika had picked up a variegated scent on the breeze, and she knew what they'd find when they circled the block to the training ground enclosed behind it.

Quick.

She was kneeling at the edge of the building inside the shaded curve of its wings. Every so often she plunged a sponge into a bucket of soapy water, then used it to scrub the breeze blocks clean, muttering to herself irritably the whole time.

Kulika pulled the doctor to a stop at the corner of the building, where they could peek around into the courtyard without being seen themselves.

'Why are you—'

Kulika interrupted Dr Ross by revealing her silver, letting the doctor see how the silver in the whites of her eyes had extended into her irises: the physical mark of her feelings for Quick.

'Oh,' Dr Ross said. Then she nodded towards Quick and said, 'Her?'

'Her,' Kulika confirmed. 'I wouldn't still be in this place if she could be anywhere else.'

'*Oh,*' Dr Ross said again, her expression pained now. 'The baron mentioned something about a covenant?'

'She signed it,' Kulika confirmed. 'Under duress.'

Dr Ross was a clever woman. She understood the rest without Kulika having to spell it out.

Standing across the training ground from Quick without being able to approach her was an exquisite kind of torture. Kulika could smell the scent of lush blackberries, sharp spring daffodils and frost-rimed rose-hips rolling across the space towards her, making her wish for nothing more than to carry Quick back across the Atlantic with her and undress her underneath the first convenient hedgerow. She'd settle for undressing her under the Spanish moss hanging from the mansion's oak trees if that option was available to her, but the doctor was standing right beside her, and besides, she didn't have permission from Bartholomew to be here right now. If he found Kulika with Quick then she was certain he'd make her pay for that liberty, in blood or in shame.

'Come on,' Kulika said quietly to the doctor. 'I'll walk you to the truck.'

In that moment, Quick's head snapped up and froze in place, like she'd just heard something. She couldn't have heard Kulika speaking, though. She'd pitched her voice so that it would only carry to Dr Ross, and anyway Quick was so new that her hearing wouldn't be that sensitive yet. Would it?

Then Quick turned her head a little to the side and sniffed the air. God, could she *smell* Kulika? Even from across the training ground, with the breeze moving away from her?

Quick turned a little further around and locked eyes with Kulika, before shifting her gaze to the doctor, then back to Kulika.

'Kulika,' Quick said. There was something bleak in her eyes, but Kulika couldn't afford to hang around and find out what it was. She'd already lingered here too long.

'Quick,' Kulika murmured, then she nudged the doctor back towards the drive, where Enzo would be waiting with the truck.

She should never have come out here in the first place. Bartholomew would know, as he always knew, and would always know.

Perhaps it was time Kulika did something about that.

17

QUICK'S EXCURSION WITH Bella the previous day should have been more exciting than it had proved to be. Mansion-hunting around South Carolina was certainly better than scrubbing the toilets in the block, but Bella hadn't been kidding when she'd said that Quick would be her chauffeur. Quick had driven up to the grand gateways of any number of gorgeous houses, but she'd been ordered to stay in the car every time. Given her sun allergy, perhaps that had been a blessing in disguise.

Bella had thrown her sunglasses onto the console angrily the moment she'd sashayed her way back into the SUV after the third viewing, and said, 'You know they all do this, right?'

Quick'd had no idea what she was talking about.

'Everyone back at the house who's ever turned someone Silver has done it by pretending to be someone they're not,' Bella had continued. As she'd spoken, she'd twisted the silver locket she'd been wearing, tightening its fine chain around her own throat. 'Enzo, Monty, Kulika, all of them. And because they all do it, they pretend like that makes it okay. Maybe it *does*. Maybe the only way to deal with that is by following their example.'

Bella's anger had mellowed as she'd talked her way through this, apparently not requiring any input from Quick, who might as well have been invisible.

Quick should have worried more about that at the time, but instead her mind had got stuck on the first bit of what Bella had said: *Everyone back at the house who's ever turned someone Silver has done it by pretending to be someone they're not.*

Driving back from Charleston on her own that evening, Quick had been sorely tempted to barrel straight past the mansion and never turn back. It had been a fleeting thought, the spontaneous impulse of a second, and she hadn't needed more than a couple of breaths to banish it.

They would find her. They would drag her back here. They would kill her, leaving Evita and Xiaoyu with no one fighting their corner at all.

So she'd discarded the idea almost as soon as it had occurred, turned sedately onto the long driveway and parked the SUV neatly in the line of vehicles that was arrayed in front of the house. Then she'd returned obediently to the block, where a long list of chores had already been awaiting her attention. She hadn't given another thought to Bella and the greasy realtor whose house she'd left her at. They'd had a tedious day driving from one tacky mansion to another, with one tedious realtor after another. Why Bella had decided to take that last one to a bar, of all the sleazy bastards they'd met that day, Quick had no idea.

But Bella had insisted she'd be fine, and Quick knew she was more than capable of looking after herself with a single middle-aged human, so she'd driven away and left Bella to her revenge sex, assuming she'd make her own way back to the mansion when she'd got it out of her system. Nothing to worry about.

Until now, that was.

'You're *sure* she hasn't been back today?' Quick asked Monty, who was glaring at her like she'd just lost a beloved pet.

'You think I don't know where my own people are?'

'I think Bella doesn't think she's one of *your* people,' Quick argued. 'I think she probably wanted to feel like her own person for a while. I'm sure she'll be back soon. She just needed some time on her own.'

'Because of Enzo,' Monty said.

'Right.'

'But otherwise she seemed perfectly fine to you yesterday?'

'Well, she wasn't *happy*,' Quick admitted.

Monty gave her a frank look. 'Bartholomew was there. From what he told me, she was more than *not happy*.'

'Okay, she was fucking livid,' Quick snapped. 'What do you expect me to say?'

'Enzo says she's crazy.'

Quick laughed. 'Right. You know what they say about men who tell you their exes are crazy?'

'What?'

'You should ask what the guy did to *drive* them crazy. He told her he loved her, then turned her Silver, dumped her and went off with his boyfriend without telling her. So is she crazy, or is she justifiably pissed off and paranoid? She wanted to blow off a little steam. I didn't see any harm in that, plus she outranks me, so what did you expect me to do?'

'Drop fifty points and go scrub the training ground walls,' Monty replied without missing a beat. '*That's* what I expect you to do.'

'But I haven't done anything wrong!' Quick protested.

Monty disagreed.

It wasn't like Quick had a right of appeal in this place, so she trudged off to the cleaning cupboard and dragged out all the supplies she'd need. While she was at it, she searched the cupboard for matches and solvents and firelighters. After checking every precariously-packed nook, she gained a Bic lighter and a nearly-empty can of lighter fluid from a box of barbecue equipment on the top shelf. It wasn't much, but it would do.

The weight of the fuel was heavy in Quick's pocket as she scrubbed away the blood that had congealed on the breeze blocks outside. They'd be able to smell the solvent on her, probably. If she wanted to use the stuff, she'd either have to stash it somewhere safe until she was ready to start the fire, or she'd have to do it immediately. The problem was, to create the distraction that would divert Bartholomew's attention away from the block long enough to get Quick into the basement, she'd have to create *another* distraction that would divert Monty and the others long enough to get Quick up to the house to start the fire in the first place.

And it would have to be up at the house, she'd decided. It was old, there was a lot of wood and polish inside, and Quick was pretty sure it would go up like kindling. It was also Bartholomew's home, so the stakes would be high enough to get everyone involved and away from the block, so she could do her thing. But with higher stakes came higher punishment, so she'd also have to make it look like an accident.

It had to be tonight, then. There'd doubtless be another pool party, and if Quick could wangle an invitation then maybe she could accidentally arrange for a cigarette to get knocked under the porch and onto an area that had somehow become soaked in lighter fluid. With any luck, the porch would hide the first flames from sight, and the party would keep anyone from noticing that anything was wrong until the fire had already properly caught hold.

Was it a great plan? Probably not. Was it the only one Quick had? Absolutely, so she was going to go with it and hope like hell it didn't blow up in her face.

Kulika.

For a moment, Quick didn't understand why the echo had suddenly popped into her mind. She'd been obsessing over the woman since... Well, since Quick had first seen her last week, if she was being honest, but usually the little pangs of want that struck her from time to time came on the heels of a thought about Kulika. They didn't just appear out of nowhere when she was in the middle of planning an arson attack.

But there it was again, that little pull, like sunshine on seawater.

Then Quick realised it was a scent that was calling her. She put down her sponge and sniffed the air, trying to work out whether the scent was real or imaginary.

Oh, it was definitely real, and it was stronger now, licking up Quick's nostrils and down her throat, making her shudder in ways she'd rather not admit, even to herself. She turned from her work, trying to track the scent.

'Kulika,' Quick said.

She was standing at the far corner of the training ground next to a short woman Quick didn't recognise, but they didn't stay. The moment Kulika locked eyes with Quick, she turned and escorted the other woman away, leaving Quick bewildered and a little hurt.

It was a nothing encounter.

Was she being surveilled? Was Kulika keeping an eye on

her?

There was no way to know.

Quick wanted to wallow in the uncertainty of it. She wanted to dissect every interaction she'd ever had with Kulika and pin down her reactions, in a vain attempt to work out where she stood. Instead, she forced her mind back to the wall, to the blood, and to the lighter fuel in her pocket. These things were tangible and real, and one of them would get Xiaoyu out of the cellar, even if Kulika Yadav would not.

18

IT HAD BEEN a mistake for Kulika to see Quick. Bartholomew gave Kulika a stern look when she returned to the house after leaving Dr Ross in Enzo's hopefully-safe hands, then he grilled her on the baron's plans and what she'd found in Jamaica. Kulika obfuscated on both, with limited success.

No, she didn't know exactly what Dr Ross was doing in the lab or why. No, she hadn't brought Bayly in, but someone had told her where he'd be at midday. Those statements weren't technically lies, but they weren't the whole truth either, and Bartholomew could tell. He let her leave for the meet with Bayly, though not without reminding her that he held Quick's life in his hands.

'You're lucky that I'm preoccupied with arrangements for phase two today,' he told her. 'I'm choosing to trust you, as my Second, to deal with these matters appropriately. Don't betray that trust, Kulika. You know what the consequences might be.'

Under the circumstances, that was more than she'd hoped for, but it meant the deal Bayly had offered her was off the table. Evita's blood wasn't enough. She needed to bring him and Evita in, and she needed to do it today.

There was still an hour before midday, so she headed to BioSilver to make sure Dr Ross had everything prepared for when Kulika returned with the blood. Kulika had been here a couple of times before, on business for the baron, which gave her the credentials to get inside. It was where the man Kulika couldn't stop thinking of as *the* Primus – Solomon – conducted the kind of research he'd rather not allow in his own territory: bioweapons, Silver poisons, and more idiosyncratic formulae like the one Enzo had stolen. The lab's distance from London gave Solomon plausible deniability, and a twelve-hour buffer in case something dangerous got loose. It was attached to one of the local universities, masquerading as a science block on a campus that didn't offer undergraduate science courses. That was an oddity, but there were enough postgraduate students that the facility passed under the radar. Solomon was good at keeping it that way.

Enzo's own lab was enormous. No wonder he didn't mind sharing with Dr Ross; there was enough white space filled with enough strange machinery to keep a whole team of biochemists busy. The door had a little plaque on it that said *Dr Enzo Cappelli*, so he'd clearly got his feet properly under the table at BioSilver. That was incredible when you thought about it, because surely a lab run by the Silver would have protocols in place to make sure they knew who they were hiring, or at the very least whether they were human or not. Somehow, Enzo had slithered his way through the net.

Kulika suspected he had form for that.

'Hi, Dr Ross,' Kulika said as she pushed through the doors to the lab. 'Are you settling in all right?'

'Oh, yes,' the doctor said. She was sitting at a work bench, looking through what Kulika assumed was a microscope at what she assumed was the formula Dr Ross had brought with her. There was an open vial on the bench next to her, in a rack holding four other identical vials. 'The lab is remarkably well equipped,' the doctor added, then she rattled off the names of a few machines that she hadn't expected the lab to have, but it was like a foreign language to Kulika. She couldn't make head nor tail of it, but then she'd never had the patience for that kind of work.

'Okay, well,' Kulika said, 'I'm going to collect the blood sample and bring it right back here. Do you have everything you need to start making the antidote?'

'I should do,' Dr Ross said, shifting a few things around on her work surface, as though she were counting things off in her head. 'Yes. I think we're ready. Has the sample been refrigerated?'

'I don't know,' said Kulika. 'Does it matter?'

'Maybe, maybe not. Hard to say without knowing how long ago the sample was drawn, or how Dr Evita Khalyed's particular pathology works, and that's if she even carries the same traits as Dr *Jahan* Khalyed did. It's a bit of a gamble. Here,' Dr Ross pulled a small cooler out from under the bench. 'Put it in this as soon as you have it. I don't suppose…' The doctor hesitated.

'Suppose what?'

'Is she okay?' Dr Ross said, looking up at Kulika with big eyes. 'Evita, I mean? I knew her grandfather, and… Well, this situation where you're bringing me a blood sample instead of the woman herself. It doesn't fill me with confidence.'

'I know. I'm trying my best here. I've got a lot of reasons to find her and see her safe, believe me.'

'Okay,' Dr Ross said after a moment.

'I'll get going, then.' Kulika held up the cooler in farewell, and made for the door.

'Oh,' Dr Ross said, 'by the way, your friend came by.'

'You mean Enzo?' Kulika asked. 'I hate to break it to you, Dr Ross, but he's not my friend. In fact, I'm pretty sure that Enzo's only real friend is Enzo.'

'No, not Enzo. The woman. The one with the generous... um, assets.' At first, Kulika thought maybe the doctor was talking about Quick, but then she added, 'The blonde one,' and Kulika started paying attention.

'What blonde one?' she asked.

'The lab assistant. Emma?' Dr Ross said vaguely, her attention half on her computer screen. 'No, Bella. That was it.'

'Bella is not my friend,' Kulika said, remembering the woman who had read the charges at Alex's execution.

The doctor looked up from her work then.

'She isn't?' Dr Ross asked.

'No. In fact, I've never even spoken to her. Are you *sure* it was Bella?'

'Long blonde hair, curvy, well-endowed, you know. Conventionally attractive, if you like that sort of thing,' Dr Ross added, in a tone that suggested she didn't, though her pink cheeks told a different story.

Oh, god.

Kulika could see how it would have been. Bella used to work at BioSilver, didn't she? That was where Enzo had met her, if Kulika remembered right. She'd been his key into the place, and now she'd waltzed back in here, charmed the eminently charmable Dr Ross, and used that access to... what?

'Are you missing anything?' Kulika asked, looking around to see if anything was out of place. 'Did she take something from the lab?'

'No, of course not,' the doctor replied, affronted. 'She was barely in here five minutes. We just had a little chat and then — Oh.' Her gaze had landed on the vials at her elbow. 'Um.'

'Um?' Kulika said sharply.

'Well, um. There were six of those, and now… But surely not. I must have knocked one out of the holder, or left one in the cool box when I lifted them out. Check the— Check the cool box.' Dr Ross was getting jittery now, her hand shaking a little as she pointed at the cooler Kulika was holding.

Kulika opened it, emptied it out, turned it upside down. 'Nothing,' she said.

'Oh, dear,' Dr Ross said, taking off her glasses and chewing at one of the arms. Then she popped beneath the work bench, searching the floor, and popped up again with her hair half undone and anxiety written all over her face. 'Oh, dear,' she said again.

'Remind me what that formula does?' Kulika asked, as calmly as she could.

'It, um.' The doctor licked her lips. 'If injected into Dr Evita Khalyed, it would probably turn her into the same kind of monster that Jahan became. He, um, whenever he bit one of the Silver – which the formula seemed to *make* him do – the people he bit went up in smoke, burning up instantly from the inside out.'

'And if anyone else took it?'

'Someone human? I don't know. We haven't done the tests. But someone Silver? They'd probably…' The doctor pushed the hair out of her eyes and put her glasses back on. 'They'd just die, I think. The same way as when Jahan bit people. Burned up.'

Kulika took a deep breath and let it out again slowly.

'So what you're telling me,' she said, 'is that Bella has her hands on a vial of poison that will kill any Silver she chooses to give it to.'

'Yes,' the doctor said in a small voice.

'How long ago did she leave?' Kulika asked, already packing the cooler up again and heading for the door.

'About half an hour, I suppose?'

'I have to go and get the bloody blood sample. You keep looking for the vial, just in case. I'll call Bartholomew.'

Dr Ross paled. 'Do you have to—'

'There's a rogue Silver out there with a Silver-killing weapon. She's a member of his crew. She's signed his covenant. Yes, I have to call Bartholomew.'

The doctor nodded hopelessly.

'I'll be back with the blood sample,' Kulika promised, 'then we'll sort this out. Sit tight.'

Bloody newbies.

Kulika had told Bartholomew that it was a bad idea to have all these new, untested Silver running around barely supervised. It wasn't just the physical changes either, it was the mental ones. Turning into what they were could change your whole perception of the world and your place in it, and the way Bartholomew was gathering them all together into this cult of his was enough to fuck anyone up. It certainly seemed to have fucked Bella up, good and proper, but saying *I told you so* wasn't going to get Kulika very far right now, particularly when she'd been the one who'd brought Dr Ross here with the killer formula in the first place.

When she called Bartholomew, she stuck to the facts, and they were bad enough. He didn't yell. Kulika would have felt better if he'd yelled.

Christ.

If it wasn't one disaster, it was another.

And then, inevitably, another.

Bayly wasn't waiting for Kulika on the pier at midday.

Instead, she found Enzo there, sitting on one of the wide wooden benches and looking across the harbour to Fort Sumter.

'He's not coming,' Kulika said.

'No,' Enzo agreed. 'He gave me the blood, though. Here.'

Enzo passed over a large, conspicuously un-refrigerated vial. Kulika sighed and stowed it away in the cooler.

'Where is he, Enzo?'

'I don't know,' he replied, his eyes fixed on the dolphins cruising through the harbour.

'I don't believe you. You know I have to take you both back to the mansion. I have to bring Evita too, sooner or later, but if I show up with you on your own then Bartholomew's just going to kill you to wipe out Bayly. He's ruthless like that, and he doesn't like being messed around. I don't either, especially by people who are supposed to be my friends.'

'We're not friends,' Enzo said, in a horrified tone that Kulika might have found it offensive if she wasn't so angry.

'I wasn't talking about you, you pillock. I was talking about Bayly. Now where is he, and what's he done with Evita Khalyed?'

Enzo still said nothing.

'I don't know what he sees in you,' Kulika said. She turned to face Enzo, then rested one foot on the bench where he was sitting, so she loomed over him. 'I can understand what you would see in him, if you actually gave a shit about him at all, which I think is unlikely. I think you're a slimy little opportunist, Enzo. I think you're under the impression that you're going to walk away from this, but let me set you straight on that.'

Kulika moved her foot quickly, landing it squarely in Enzo's crotch and pinning him to the bench with the heel of her boot. The noise he made was satisfyingly high-pitched. He wriggled and squirmed and tried to break free, but Kulika knew her craft and she was significantly stronger than him.

'If you don't tell me where Bayly is right now, I'm going to drag you back to the mansion and hand you over to Bartholomew. He will not be kind. I might not be either,' she said, grinding her heel a little to reinforce her message.

'He bought a boat,' Enzo squeaked.

'Where?'

'The marina by the aquarium.'

'Name?'

'*Buried Treasure.*'

'Of course it is. Christ, Enzo,' Kulika said, finally removing her foot, 'you could have told me this yesterday. You knew I was going to Jamaica looking for Evita.'

Enzo hunched over and moaned for a moment before replying. 'I do have some loyalty, you know.'

Kulika scoffed. 'You could've fooled me.'

'Yeah, well, I was dealing with problems of my own yesterday. Bella got all emotional on me. Apparently she thought me turning her meant more than it did. She got upset. You know.'

Kulika's temper flared.

'You know she's stolen a vial of formula from the lab now?' she said.

'What?' Enzo asked. 'Why?'

'Not the formula that makes turning Silver easier – you already stole that out from under BioSilver's nose. I'm talking about the formula Dr Ross brought with her from the UK.'

Enzo blanched.

'I guess you know what it does, then?'

'Look,' he said evasively, 'how could I have known she'd

react like that? I didn't expect her to go all cuckoo on me. I needed her to trust me so I could get into BioSilver, so I needed to turn her Silver, which meant, you know…'

'You led her on.'

'Barely,' Enzo insisted. 'I'm gay.'

'Did you tell her that?'

'Of course not.'

'Then what does it have to do with anything?'

'Why are you looking at me like this is my fault? Maybe I gave her a slightly false impression so I could get into BioSilver like Bartholomew wanted, but none of this is on me. How was I supposed to know she was a fucking maniac?'

Kulika couldn't believe what she was hearing, but she knew from her long experience dealing with killer Silver – mostly men, mostly narcissistic, never willing to admit their mistakes – that a man with so little conscience couldn't be made to see the error of his ways. Her time and irritation would be better spent focusing on the immediate problem: Bayly.

Bartholomew had assured her he'd deal with Bella – possibly the worst call Kulika had ever had to make – but he'd also assured her that there'd be trouble if she wasn't back that afternoon with Enzo and Bayly in tow.

'Come on,' she said, dragging Enzo to his feet. 'We're going for an afternoon out at the aquarium.'

19

SOMEONE WAS BANGING pans together inside the block. At first, Quick thought it was just bad cookery, but it soon became clear that the noise was meant to be an alarm call of some kind. She could hear people filtering through the corridors, so she abandoned her sponge and bucket and followed them to the big common room to find out what was going on.

Brandon was standing on a chair by the board.

'We need volunteers!' he yelled as everyone crowded into the room. 'Two hundred points up for grabs!'

'For what?' someone shouted.

'We got a rogue,' Brandon replied. 'One of the crew's gone missing.'

Quick's stomach sank. She was pretty sure she knew who he was talking about.

'Who?' someone else yelled.

'Bella,' said Monty. He was standing beside Brandon's chair, and he was looking directly at Quick.

Shit.

'Fuck, no,' someone said, turning and leaving the room. He wasn't the only one, either. As soon as the crowd heard that it was Bella who was missing, half of them made a swift exit.

'She's crazy,' one of the remaining Silver said. 'Where's the danger money?'

'Four hundred, then,' Brandon said.

The guy who'd spoken considered this for a moment, then said, 'Nah. The others are right. It's not worth it,' and walked away.

Quick made to follow him and the others out of the room when Monty caught her wrist and dragged her back.

'Not so quick there, Quick,' he said, with little humour. 'Something tells me this is the perfect job for you. After all, you're the one who lost her.'

'I didn't lose her,' Quick replied, trying and failing to snatch her hand back. 'I told you: she's just blowing off steam. Where's the harm?'

'Where's the *harm*?' Monty said patronisingly. 'The harm is that this morning, Bella walked back into the BioSilver labs using her old security pass, and into the office where Enzo works.'

'Oh no,' said Quick, getting a bad feeling in the pit of her stomach.

'Where Bella found a visiting doctor using Enzo's equipment,' Monty continued as if she hadn't spoken, 'and pretended she was his lab assistant to get into the lab and lay her hands on, well, whatever she could find.'

'Oh no,' Quick said again.

'Which happened to be a formula that the visiting doctor had brought with her to develop an antidote for a dangerous and contagious Silver virus. Or poison. Or whatever. I don't exactly know, but the point is that Bella's now out there, running around pissed at Enzo and Bartholomew and probably the rest of us too, and she's got her hands on a vial of stuff that could actually kill us. So yeah. *Oh no.*'

'And you're trying to blame this on me?' Quick said incredulously. 'I'm three days old, remember? And bottom of the board.'

'You could go lower,' Monty said threateningly. 'So where is she?'

'How the hell am I supposed to know?' Quick said irritably. 'She had me drive her from one realtor's office to another, and we looked at some properties, but apparently none of them were right. Then she asked me to drive her and this one realtor to a bar, which I did, and then I dropped them back at his place in North Charleston. She said she was going to get a lift home.'

'Where's the house?'

Which was a reasonable question, to which Quick had no answer. She'd used the satnav, and she didn't know that area well. She couldn't remember exactly where they'd been.

'Can you check the trip history on the SUV's computer?' she suggested.

'No, but I'll tell you what: *you* can.'

For a moment, Quick didn't understand what he was suggesting.

'You want me to go after her?' she asked. '*Me?*'

'Well, you can use Silver speed now, and if what I saw the other night is anything to go by, you're pretty good with your hands, too.' He smirked.

Quick seethed. 'You were *watching* us?'

It wasn't as though she and Kulika had done anything out on the training ground except fight and talk, but the idea that Monty had been spying on them was unsettling and intrusive. It had Quick running through her memory of the night in her head, trying to find anything he might have misconstrued, and she hated that. It had been *her* night with

Kulika, maybe the last one she'd get. However badly it had ended, there'd been parts of it that she'd cherish for as long as she lived. It didn't belong to Monty. She didn't want his grubby little fingerprints on any of it.

'*Everyone* was watching,' Monty said. 'How do you think you got bumped up the board ten places?'

'I didn't know.' Quick hadn't looked at the board since she'd first found out about it. 'I didn't think I'd earned any points.'

'Well, here's your chance to earn some more,' Monty said.

'Come on, Monty,' said Brandon, hopping down from the chair. 'It's not like the newbie's going to be able to overpower Bella.'

'And then you're wasting our only lead,' Penny chimed in, the only other Silver who'd hung around. 'She'll tip Bella off, then it'll be that much harder for us to find her later.'

'Four hundred, if you bring her in,' Monty said to Quick, ignoring the others. 'Another two hundred if you bring back the vial, unopened.'

'The vial that'll kill me?' Quick asked. 'No way.' Then she thought for a moment and said, 'Not on my own.'

Which was how she, Brandon and Penny ended up on a road trip to North Charleston. Quick was playing chauffeur again while Brandon lounged in the passenger seat and Penny sprawled in the back.

There was a buzz, and Brandon pulled his phone out of his pocket.

'Message from Monty,' he explained. 'He's spoken to Bella on the phone.'

'Did he find out where she is?' Penny asked.

'No, but he warned her about the vial thing being a poison. Apparently she thinks it's some kind of cure. That's what the doctor told her.'

'A cure for what?' Penny asked.

'Not sure. Monty says she hung up on him, and now her phone's off.'

'So the plan stays the same?'

'I guess.'

The plan, such as it was, was to use the satnav to return to the last place Quick had seen Bella, then have a poke about. It shouldn't have worked. It had been nearly twenty-four hours ago that Quick had left Bella here, and she could have gone anywhere with that long a head start, but when Quick parked up in front of the realtor's quaint little house and they all spilled out of the SUV, the first thing Brandon said was, 'Her scent's here.'

'How recent?' Penny asked.

'Recent. Like, maybe she's still here. Let's send the newbie to knock on the door and see.'

Quick didn't like being called *the newbie*, but she disliked the vibes surrounding the house even more. She really, *really* didn't want to knock on the door, but they were going to have to do it sooner or later. Pulling the band-aid off as fast as possible had always been Quick's preferred approach, so she opened her parasol before she could talk herself out of it and went to knock on the pretty stained-glass-windowed door.

Part of her had been expecting it to swing open, but that didn't happen. She tried the handle.

'Locked,' she called back at Brandon and Penny, but they'd already moved to the side door next to the garage.

'This one isn't,' Penny called back.

When Quick joined them, she saw that not only was the door not locked, but the lock had been pushed clean through the doorframe.

'Well, that's not good,' said Brandon, hanging back to

examine the door while Penny went into the garage. The space was L-shaped, with enough room for a car up front, and a work bench along the back wall. The section that continued off to one side to join the main house looked like a utility space, but because of the shape of the room, Quick couldn't see much except the edge of a chest freezer from where she was standing with Brandon. Penny had walked all the way to the back wall though, so she could see plenty.

She screeched and jumped back.

'What?' Brandon asked, but Penny didn't pay him any attention. Instead, she was backing slowly away from the utility area, her eyes wide and fixed on the hidden area in front of her.

'Penny!' Brandon yelled sharply, to get her attention. 'What gives?'

Finally, she looked at Brandon with haunted eyes, pointed into the utility space and said, 'What the hell are *they*?'

20

THE *BURIED TREASURE* was an unassuming little motorboat with a single small cabin. Kulika had imagined that, after all his centuries, Bayly might have been able to afford a yacht, or even a super-yacht, but then he'd always refused to invest in property because he didn't want to be tied to dry land. If all you did was buy boat after boat, assets which depreciated over time, then your bank balance sank along with them. It was clearly a lesson Bayly had resolutely failed to learn.

It made Kulika's job easier though, as did the fact that the marina was deserted.

'Bayly!' she yelled, dragging Enzo out of the backseat of the car where he'd sat obediently the whole way from Waterfront Park. Now that she'd shown him what she could do, he wasn't even trying to challenge her physically. It was clear that Enzo's arsenal – such as it was – was entirely emotional: he was a lover, not a fighter.

'If you want to live,' Kulika yelled, 'you'll step out of the boat and into the car without a fight.'

'You wouldn't kill me, Kulika,' came a voice from inside the cabin. 'I'm crew.'

'And Bartholomew has Quick,' Kulika reminded him. 'I think what I'd do for her might surprise us both. Do you want to test me and see, or do you want to come with me voluntarily and have at least some chance of surviving this?'

Bayly laughed as he finally emerged from the cabin. 'What Bartholomew will do to me if I go back to the mansion will surprise neither of us. I'm dead either way.'

'I'm his Second now,' Kulika argued. 'I can put in a good word.'

Bayly just shook his head. 'Face it, Kulika. I gambled it all to get me and Enzo out of here, and I lost.' Then his gaze shifted sideways to land on his boyfriend, frozen in Kulika's grip. 'He still didn't want to leave.'

Kulika looked between the two men, confused until Bayly explained further.

'We were supposed to trade the girl for Enzo's freedom from the covenant, but then you came along and spoiled that. Then we were supposed sail off into the sunset together and leave the girl behind on the pier for you to find this afternoon, hoping that Bartholomew would be too distracted with his plans to come after us, but Enzo still didn't want to go. Now we're both going to die because he can't stop dreaming of Bartholomew's glorious Silver future.'

'It's not a dream, Bayly,' Enzo said plaintively. 'It's *reality* and it's coming. Just a few more days, and you'll see.'

Bayly had the long-suffering expression of someone who'd been through this argument a hundred time before.

'We won't see,' he said, 'because we'll be dead.'

'Then go!' Enzo yelled. 'But I'm a part of it, and I'm staying.'

'And if I leave without you then he'll kill you just to take me off the board.'

'No, he won't,' Enzo insisted.

'Actually,' Kulika said, 'I think he probably will.'

'See?' Bayly said, but Enzo clearly wasn't listening. It was as though he'd plugged up his ears with all of Bartholomew's nonsense, and there must have been a lot of it in Enzo's head to get him to rob BioSilver in the first place. It wasn't a minor crime. Even Kulika would have thought twice about stealing from Solomon, and then she would probably have decided it wasn't worth it in the end. To get a young Silver like Enzo to agree to do something so reckless must have involved a serious degree of brainwashing.

But then Bartholomew was an expert at that.

'Academic now, anyway,' Kulika said. 'I've been ordered to bring you both in, so that's what's going to happen.'

'Dead or alive?' Bayly said.

'Preferably alive.'

'His preference or yours?'

'Both, I guess.'

'And mine,' said Enzo to Bayly. 'Let's make it alive, please.'

Bayly didn't seem inclined to agree, an inclination he proved when the boat's engine churned to life.

'Don't you dare, Bayly!' Kulika yelled.

She knocked Enzo out so he wouldn't go anywhere, then rushed towards the boat. She found Bayly in the cabin, downing bottles of blood from a cooler by the bed. It was the last resort of a man who knew he couldn't beat her in a fair fight, but even when he was fuelled up on blood, it took Kulika less than ten seconds to swipe a knife from the counter and stick it through his skull.

He'd recover, but he'd be out for at least twelve hours with a brain injury like that. Longer, if she didn't take the knife out. She left it where it was, turned off the boat's engine and took a good look around the cabin.

The space was kitted out with all kinds of mod-cons, which is only what Kulika would have expected from Bayly. He'd always been a crafty sort. There was a kitchen counter along one side, where she'd found the knife. It was equipped with all kinds of clever space-saving designs, like a fold-out breakfast bar and folding chairs that stacked away into the space beneath it. The whole thing looked bespoke, probably hand-crafted by Bayly himself. On the other side of the cabin was a bed, which looked for all the world like just a bed: a double mattress tucked against the wall on a raised divan. No drawers, no clever foldaway furniture, no storage, and that wasn't like Bayly at all.

Kulika lifted the entire mattress off the bed, meaning to take a look underneath, which is when she realised that it had been designed to lift in precisely that way. Gas struts kicked into action, raising the mattress off the divan on a platform of slats, like a drawbridge raising to reveal the moat beneath, or certainly something that smelled like a moat. It was a lead box, about a yard along each side, encrusted with sand and barnacles. Inside, Kulika could hear the faintest thud: a slow, erratic pulse.

This was the box that Bayly had kept buried in the Palisadoes for so many centuries, Kulika was certain. It smelled of salt and age and the kind of rank odours that attach to a place that's been used as a graveyard. All that, plus blood. A lot of blood. Old and curdled and rotten blood that had kept dead things alive beyond the point at which they should have long decayed.

Kulika looked around the room, her eyes skipping over Bayly's blood-soaked body, until she spotted a toolbox stowed under the edge of the counter. Inside, she found a couple of screwdrivers that she used to pry the edge off the box and lift the lid.

Almost immediately, she wished she hadn't. The stench that rose from within was like nothing Kulika had ever smelled before. It scorched the insides of her nostrils with ammonia and putrescence, making her eyes water until she had to dash the tears away to see inside the damned thing.

The first thing she saw was the woman. She was blood-stained and barely conscious, and so thin she was practically emaciated, but Kulika had no doubt that this was Dr Evita Khalyed. She'd changed, but not enough to stop Kulika from recognising her from her picture. Her eyes were closed, but she was alive, barely.

Then Kulika noticed the black vines that had wrapped their way around Evita's hips, shoulders and throat, tightening into her skin until they strangled her flesh in their grip. It was while Kulika was trying to work out how to extricate her from the off-puttingly moist tendrils around her throat that she noticed a round mass attached to Evita's neck. She leaned in to examine it more closely. There was something wrong with the shape, something familiar and yet twisted about its construction that set alarm bells clanging in the back of her head.

Then two white circles snapped into existence in the black morass. The part of the black shape closest to Evita's neck pulled away like a snail's foot writhing in the air for purchase, revealing the teeth that were sunk into Evita's skin.

'Shit!' Kulika yelled, dropping the screwdrivers as she jumped back in fright.

The figure that she'd initially mistaken for a growth of slimy black vines started unwrapping itself from around Evita's body, then it pulled itself slowly out of the box, bone by blackened bone. Its jaw gaped open to reveal a tongueless mouth. Parts of its skull were caved in and misshapen, to the degree that it surely wasn't capable of conscious thought. It couldn't walk. It couldn't stand, but it could drag itself over the lip of the box one barely-connected piece at a time, leading with teeth that snapped rapaciously in Kulika's direction.

She could put two and two together now: Bayly hadn't just buried Evita in the same place as he'd buried his old boyfriend over three hundred years ago. He'd buried her in the same bloody box.

By the time she'd got over the shock of that realisation, the skeletal oil slick was dragging itself towards Bayly's unconscious body, having honed in on the easier prey of the two of them. It took Kulika a moment to get Evita's body out of the box, long enough that when she returned to wrestle the Digs creature back into the box and seal it in, it had already taken a chunk out of Bayly's leg.

She figured that was the least he owed him.

'Shit,' Kulika panted to herself as she bent the edges of the lead box closed again and slammed the mattress back down on top of the divan. She heard movement behind her and swivelled, thinking maybe one of those horrible grasping hands had become detached and got left behind, but it was just Evita Khalyed, pushing herself weakly up from the floor. Kulika gave her a hand up on to the mattress, where she'd not only be more comfortable, but could also give Kulika some extra reassurance that the sticky skeletal bastard wasn't going to get back out again.

Jane, Kulika reminded herself. *She thinks her name is Jane.*

'Jane,' she said gently, 'I know you don't know me, but —'

'Evita,' she whispered.

Kulika froze. 'Excuse me?'

'My name's Evita,' she coughed weakly. 'Dr Evita Khalyed.'

'You remember?'

Evita tried to laugh, but ended up hunched over herself as she coughed and coughed. Kulika tried to offer her a drink of blood from one of the bottles in Bayly's cooler, but Evita just coughed it right back out again. The coughing fit was taking so long to subside that Kulika was considering cutting a hole in the woman's throat to pour the stuff straight in. The wound would heal quickly enough, but Evita wasn't going to heal at all if she couldn't get any new blood in her system. Finally, though, she stopped coughing enough to swallow.

'I've had some time to think in there,' she whispered after she'd emptied the bottle. 'Time to remember. I wondered why I knew so much pirate history, enough to have me cruising across the Caribbean on some stupid treasure hunt — But yes,' she said, with more strength in her voice. 'I remember who I am, now.'

Kulika smiled. 'Patience Quick is going to be thrilled to hear it.'

'You know Quick?'

'Yes.' Kulika didn't want to say too much. She couldn't imagine that Evita would be pleased to hear how much her best friend had suffered in her attempts to find her. 'She's back at the mansion.'

'What do you mean, she's... She's *Silver*?' Evita's tone of voice made it clear that this would not be a good thing.

Reluctantly, Kulika said, 'Yes.'

Evita's face clouded over. 'So while I've been stuck in this box, my best friend came looking for me and got herself mixed up in my mess. Is that about right?'

Kulika shrugged helplessly.

'I'm going to kill him,' Evita said.

'Bayly's part of the crew,' said Kulika. 'I don't blame you for being angry, but…'

'*Angry*? I just spent however long locked in a box with a blood-starved skeleton from the seventeenth century. I'm not angry, I'm fucking *livid*. But not with Bayly. That was my own fault for letting Brandon and Penny drag me into their stupid treasure hunt. No, it's Bartholomew who deserves to die,' she said, brushing the dried and crusted blood from her bare arms. 'He's the one who turned me into *this*.'

For a moment, Kulika thought she must have heard wrong. She was the only person Bartholomew had ever turned Silver. She was sure of this, and had been sure of it for three hundred years. He'd never cared enough about anyone else to turn them Silver, he'd told her himself.

At least until six months ago.

The implications were troubling, but if this meant what Kulika thought it meant, then it explained why Bayly had been under the impression that he'd be able to trade Evita's freedom for his and Enzo's. And if Bayly had been planning to make that deal, couldn't Kulika make a similar one?

Oh, yes. Evita Khalyed was going to be very useful indeed.

21

THERE WERE SEVEN zombies chained up along the garage wall, and they weren't like the one Quick had seen back in the cellar.

'Why are their eyes bleeding like that?' Penny asked, her face pale and horrified. 'And why are they moving so... weird?'

The zombie in the blood cellar had moved in an almost animalistic way, snarling and snapping and hunched like a hyena. These ones were different. Instead of lunging at Penny and Brandon and Quick, they were watching them through crying eyes that streaked bloody tears down their faces. All the while they swayed together in a constant, sinuous motion, like tree branches waving in the same breeze, as though they were all part of one entity rather than individual beings.

Whatever was up with these creatures, Quick knew in her gut that it wasn't right. It made her want to turn around, get back into the SUV and drive straight to the airport, consequences be damned. Unfortunately, with Brandon and Penny here, that wasn't an option.

'Let's find Bella,' Brandon said, keeping a careful eye on

the zombies as he stepped past them, following bloody footprints through the open doorway into the house.

But Bella wasn't in the house. She wasn't in the kitchen, or in the sitting room, or in the game room, or in any of the grandly-appointed bedroom suites. Eventually, Quick found her underneath the breakfast bar, but only because she literally tripped over her.

'What's all this dust?' she said, more to herself than to the others, who were still searching upstairs. The stuff was thick and almost sticky. It coated Quick's polished leather chauffeur shoes, dulling the patent shine to a matte grey. She toed through the pile, spreading it around to see if maybe it was an ant or termite nest that had erupted through the floor, or the remains of a fire that might have left a char mark beneath it, but instead she dislodged a small, shiny object that went skittering away over the tiles.

It was a locket on a silver chain. A familiar locket, the one that Quick had noticed Bella twisting around her neck the previous day. When she scooped it up from the floor and snapped it open, there was a smarmy photo of Enzo inside. That was the kicker.

'Oh, no,' Quick murmured.

'What?' Brandon yelled from upstairs.

'I think I found Bella.'

'What?' Penny said, rushing back into the kitchen with Brandon hot on her heels. 'Where?'

Quick pointed at her feet.

'I don't know what TV shows you've been watching,' Brandon said with a laugh. 'But real vampires don't turn to ash when they die.'

'This one did,' Quick insisted. She showed him the locket, dangling it from her fingers.

'But that's not... It doesn't work like that.'

'Did you find the vial of poison?' Quick asked.

Brandon and Penny went still.

'No,' Brandon said after a moment.

'Maybe that's how it works with the poison,' Quick said, pointing to a suspiciously vial-shaped piece of broken glass on the countertop. She'd missed it in the first search, because there was a lot of glass in the kitchen, mostly broken beer bottles. There was a lot of blood, too, some of it on the broken vial.

'Don't touch it,' Penny said.

'I wasn't going to.'

'Shit!' Brandon yelled, looking from the pile of ash to the broken vial to the zombies who were leering at them through the open door to the garage. 'What's the story, then? She got so pissed with Enzo that she killed herself?'

'Or she was trying to turn her first Silver and got depressed after failing seven times in a row?' Penny suggested. 'That would explain the zombies.'

'I don't think anything can explain *those* zombies,' said Quick.

'It's the fucking vial, isn't it?' Brandon said, letting off a stream of invective.

'She thought it was a cure,' Quick said, putting the pieces together. 'Maybe she was trying to cure the zombies with it, and instead she turned them into… whatever that is.'

'Maybe she was trying to cure herself,' Penny suggested quietly, then she turned away to wipe her eyes without Brandon noticing. Quick noticed, though.

'We'll need to take her back to the mansion, so the crew can consume her power,' said Brandon.

'I'm not eating *that*,' Penny wailed, pointing at the ash that had once been their friend.

'Then you can argue with Bartholomew about it, but

we're taking it. We need to clean the rest of this shit up, too. And be careful with that glass, newbie. Don't need you going up in smoke too.'

Quick got to work, but the ash, the broken vial and the blood and glass all over the kitchen floor weren't their only problems. There were drag marks leading from the dining area back into the garage, which Brandon followed to a body in the chest freezer.

'Oh, fuck me sideways,' Brandon yelled. 'Not another one.'

'Human,' Penny said. 'Dead. From the clothes and the gloves, he looks like the gardener.'

Which was when Quick abandoned her cleaning to take a closer look at the zombies.

'Maid service,' she said, looking at the logo on one woman's T-shirt. 'Security guard, window cleaner, HVAC technician, postal worker,' she said, listing off the other logos she could see. 'There's only two people here who aren't wearing uniforms for some kind of service. They probably all came to the house.'

'It's like Bella was sitting here and waiting for her food to just walk into her mouth,' Brandon said.

'Ugh,' Penny sneered. 'You don't have to put it like that.'

'Well, how would you put it?'

'I don't know. But not like *that*.'

Quick should have gone back to cleaning, but now that she was standing in front of the zombies again, she found she couldn't look away.

'What's wrong with them?' Penny asked.

'It looks like they're afraid of the light,' said Quick, watching how they avoided the light coming in from the high garage window. 'Maybe that's why their eyes are bleeding.'

'Yeah,' Penny said, taking a step closer so she could watch the zombies shy away. 'And it looks like they're scared of us, too.'

'Neither of those things are normal, are they?' Quick asked.

'Nope,' said Brandon. 'Nothing about this is normal.'

The three of them watched the zombies' undulations with a strange fascination. They didn't speak or howl or make any sound that even approached verbalisation, but each wave-like motion of their bodies was accompanied by the gentle clanking of chains and the continued *drip drip* of bloody tears from their chins. It was gruesome and hypnotic.

'Can we just put them out of their misery and get out of here, please?' Penny said after a while.

'Bartholomew'll want to study them,' said Brandon.

'Then he can study a dead one,' said Penny.

'Fine,' said Brandon. 'Then you stab them through the brain and I'll pile them in the back of the SUV.'

'Why can't you do the stabbing?'

'Why can't you?' Brandon argued.

'*Someone* has to do it,' said Penny.

Quick wasn't sure she agreed, but then she didn't get a vote.

'Then that someone's going to be you,' said Brandon to Penny.

'Fine!' Penny yelled.

Quick chose to absent herself during the stabbing, turning her attention instead to what remained of Bella. She found an old tea caddy in one of the kitchen cupboards, swept up the ashes with a dustpan and brush and poured the cremains into the tin.

But she was still close enough to hear the unpleasant crunch of metal on bone as the first zombie was put to rest.

Or, at least, *should have been* put to rest.

There were several more unpleasant noises, then Penny said, 'Why isn't he dying?' in a desperate, high-pitched voice.

Quick didn't mean to go and look. Truly, it was the last thing she wanted to do, but she couldn't *not* go and see for herself. Afterwards, she had a feeling she would never stop seeing the image of that broken creature, still trying to move as Penny broke one part of it after another. The injury to its head didn't make any difference at all. It didn't seem to need a brain to function.

'Fuck,' Penny said after a few more seconds' gruesome work. 'That's it. I'm done. He's not going down, and we can't put them all in the SUV like this. Call for the truck.'

'They'll dock our points,' Brandon pointed out.

'Fuck the points,' Penny replied. 'I don't want to be here anymore. Call the fucking truck.'

'Seconded,' Quick said quietly from the doorway.

Brandon called the fucking truck.

22

EVITA WAS QUIET on the drive back to the mansion, which wasn't surprising. She'd been blood-starved for months, locked in a lead box with the wraith that had once been Digs – who by all accounts hadn't been a very nice guy to begin with – and buried six feet under in the sand beneath the Palisadoes. In the circumstances, Kulika was amazed to find her capable of rational thought, but it was clear from the suspicious way she was watching Kulika that she was. Since Evita had just seen Kulika incapacitate both Bayly and Enzo, then throw their broken bodies in the back of the car, her suspicion wasn't much of a surprise.

'You're taking me back to him, aren't you?' Evita said eventually.

'For now,' Kulika admitted.

'For how long?'

'Until the weekend, maybe? By then, it'll all be over, one way or another.'

'It's happening *now*?'

Kulika glanced at Evita, wondering just how much she knew. Bartholomew's plan for the revelation must have been in play since the beginning of the year, because that's when he'd first begun gathering the Silver in numbers, and making more. In fact, thinking about the timelines, Evita might have been one of the very first Silver to be turned.

'He's in the final stages of his revelation timeline,' Kulika confirmed.

'And you're helping him?'

'I don't… Sort of.' Kulika didn't know what to say, so she just said, 'It's complicated.'

'There's a painting of you in his bedroom,' Evita said.

'Huh?' Kulika had been paying attention to the road, so it took her a moment to process the subject change. 'Whose bedroom?'

'Bartholomew's.'

'You've been in his bedroom?' Kulika asked incredulously. *No one* went in Bartholomew's bedroom. He was like a monk.

'I woke up there after I was turned,' Evita said. 'Long, irrelevant story. My concern is that you're close to him, and since he's the antichrist, that makes me reluctant to trust you.'

'I can understand that,' Kulika conceded.

'Then tell me: why should I?'

Kulika was quiet for a moment. Her first instinct was to do something incredibly ill-advised. She wanted Evita to trust her, but—

Oh, fuck it.

'Maybe I was close to Bartholomew once,' Kulika admitted. 'Maybe we're close again now, but he's not the person I care most about at the mansion.'

'No?'

'No. The person I care most about is Quick.'

Evita *humphed* dismissively. 'You've known Bartholomew hundreds of years. You can't have known

Quick longer than six months.'

'About six days, actually.'

Evita *humphed* again.

'You know about silvering?' Kulika asked.

'Yeah. Bayly and Enzo, right?'

'Not just them,' Kulika said, then she looked away from the road for a moment to reveal her silver to Evita.

The other woman went still.

Kulika looked back to the road. 'You might not be able to trust me with anything else,' she said quietly, 'but believe me when I say that you can trust me with Quick.'

'I see,' said Evita.

A minute passed in silence, after which Evita added, 'Then you'd better fill me in on everything that's happened to her since I got locked away in that box.'

23

THERE WAS PANDEMONIUM when Brandon and Penny arrived back at the mansion with a truckload of mutated zombies. It was the start of the evening pool party, so people were milling. When they heard something interesting was happening on the drive out front, they abandoned the pool and wandered around the side of the mansion in their bikinis, chasing excitement. Penny was right about one thing: they were bored.

Quick had driven the SUV back on her own, but no one was paying her any attention at all. Instead, they clustered around the back of the truck as Penny led six of the zombies out in chains and Brandon carried the seventh, who wasn't going anywhere under his own power.

'What the fuck?' someone said with revolted glee.

'The boss says to put them in the wine cellar,' said Monty, coming out of the mansion's front door. 'Through the kitchen. Come on.'

Quick wasn't going to get a better chance than this, but the distraction wouldn't last long. She had to move.

She walked casually back towards the block, passing dozens of people going in the opposite direction as they rushed to see what the commotion in the driveway was all about. That left the coast clear for her to saunter back into the wardrobe and retrieve her sweatpants from the previous day, then transfer the contents of their pockets into a loose sundress that she might reasonably choose to wear to a pool party. When she sauntered back out of the block again in her flip-flops, she was sure she looked the part, but she was also starting to get nervous.

People were already gathering poolside again, dissatisfied with the brief entertainment the new zombies had offered them. Quick had been hoping to do this next bit alone, but instead she had to pretend there was something wrong with one of her flip-flops to give her the cover she needed to bend down and empty the lighter fluid under the porch. In the end, that turned out to be a blessing – once she'd set her little fire, the broken shoe gave her an excuse to return to the block for a replacement.

No one chased her. No one raised the alarm. In fact, no one seemed to have noticed her at all. Finally, her status as newbie Silver pariah was coming in handy.

Back at the block, she ran straight to the hidden cupboard, pulling the false wall closed behind her as she lifted the hatch, with difficulty. She was stronger now, though. Strong enough, but she still couldn't see very well in the dark.

'Put the lights on, Xiaoyu,' she called softly. 'It's Quick.'

Nothing.

The cellar beneath her remained dark.

'Xiaoyu? Are you okay?'

For a moment, Quick thought maybe the humans had been moved, or – god forbid – killed, but she could hear people moving and breathing beneath her feet.

Breathing?

Maybe her senses were more attuned than she thought.

Because she was *Silver*, she reminded herself. She wasn't a prisoner in that hole anymore. She had authority that they didn't. Maybe Xiaoyu hadn't made it, but whatever was going on in the cellar, she could make the others tell her what had happened to Xiaoyu.

'I can hear you down there,' she said. 'Put the lights on. Now.'

The fluorescents blinked on and, not sure whether she was being brave or foolhardy, Quick jumped down to the dirt.

A brief survey of the space told her things had changed dramatically in the few days since she'd left. All the people were gathered down the far end, by the bathroom space, and there were about half as many as there had been before. Clearly, the Silver had been hungry.

She'd been hungry, Quick reminded herself. And this was the cost of her hunger.

But the appetites of the Silver weren't the only thing to blame for the blood bank's diminished size. In one corner, the corner nearest the hatch, there was a foul-smelling pile that Quick first mistook for rubbish bags. As she stepped closer, though, something at the edge of the pile shifted and groaned. Something with, Quick realised as she looked more closely, bleached-blonde hair and black roots.

'Xiaoyu?' Quick asked as she stepped closer, not wanting to believe the evidence of her own eyes.

The rubbish heap was a charnel pile of broken bodies and filth. Some of them were the newcomers who'd been broken when they'd been shovelled down through the hatch before the Casting, people who probably never recovered from their injuries. Others were just drained.

So many, in so few days.

And there, right at the edge, too exhausted to do much more than smile cockily at Quick, was Xiaoyu.

'She needs help!' Quick yelled at the others. 'Bring me some water.'

No one moved.

'I said, bring me some water.'

No one would meet her eye. Some even turned and started scuttling off towards the farthest corner of the cellar, or pulled themselves under their blankets like the cockroaches they were.

Xiaoyu wasn't like them. She'd guarded the hatch, and kept them safe from the zombies, and taken more than her fair share of feeds just to spare the others. She was worth more than this.

Maybe that was why Quick got so angry. Maybe she was just angry at herself.

'She looked after all of you, and you've just left her here to die,' Quick snarled. 'Well, fuck you all. You can rot down here for all I care. Come on, Xiaoyu.'

'We got sick,' one of the others said from the far side of the cellar. '*She* got sick. What were we supposed to do?'

It was a good question, but Quick didn't have an answer for it. She didn't even want to think about what the right answer might be, because she was worried that it was probably *exactly what you've done*. That would complicate things, because Quick knew very well she could probably only get one person out of this hellhole, and she wanted that person to be Xiaoyu.

Fuck complications.

She slung Xiaoyu over her shoulder and jumped up out through the hatch, slamming it shut behind her, then grabbed the bag of supplies she'd stashed in the wardrobe. If the Silver were expecting Xiaoyu to be dead any minute anyway, then surely they wouldn't miss her, which might actually give Quick the opportunity to get her off the property, once and for all.

For once, it looked like one of Quick's plans was actually working out. Behind the mansion, the eerie blue glow of the pool had been replaced with a merry orange glow coming from the porch. It was burning hard and strong, and despite a lot of activity in that area from the Silver who'd realised the mansion was on fire, it didn't look like they were having much luck putting it out.

Hopefully, it would burn the place to the ground.

Quick would come back to whatever was left. She'd have to come back to find Evita, and she was crew. The others wouldn't stop looking for her if she left, not ever. But she could get far enough away to give Xiaoyu a chance.

Quick carried her out of the block and through the trees towards the woods at the property line adjoining the road. Then Xiaoyu started coughing, and Quick had to let her rest and recover her breath so the noise didn't draw attention to their escape. Quick pulled a bottle of water out off the bag and fed it to Xiaoyu, followed by a juice box and some fruit. After that, she started to look almost human.

'What are you doing?' Xiaoyu murmured.

'First, I'm getting you away from this place,' Quick whispered, 'and then I'm putting you on a plane out of this fucking country for good.'

'No offence, Quick,' Xiaoyu groaned, 'but the only reason I have to live through this is to go back to my kids, and they're *in* this country.'

'*Kids*?'

'Yeah,' Xiaoyu said quietly. 'Kids.'

Turned out she had two of them, a boy and a girl, ten and twelve. They'd been staying with their dad while Xiaoyu had gone on holiday with her new boyfriend, but then she'd found out that the boyfriend wasn't that new after all, because he was over three hundred years old, and Silver.

'After me, the vampires chose more carefully. It's why they could never bring themselves to kill me, I guess, but they couldn't let me go, either. Not with all I know.'

'Well, they're letting you go now,' Quick said with conviction. 'You ready?'

'As I'll ever be.'

They nearly made it to the road. By that point, the fire had been quelled from flames to smoke to nothing at all. So much for Quick's plan. She could hear people moving through the woods, too, tracking her, so she opted to leave Xiaoyu for a moment to try to lead them away, but she must have got turned around at some point because she ended up bursting out of the trees onto the mansion's driveway, where a car was just pulling up.

Was that Kulika getting out of it?

Kulika.

Quick saw her circle the car until she came to the passenger door, which she opened so she could lift an unconscious figure out.

'Evita,' Quick said in disbelief, then something thudded into her from behind, pushing her face-first onto the ground. Dirt was forced up her nostrils and into her mouth, and her lungs burned with the weight on her back. She was about to throw it off and use some of the fighting techniques Kulika had shown her to get free, then there was a sharp pain in the side of her neck and spots strobed in front of her eyes.

She couldn't breathe. She didn't need to breathe, she reminded herself, but she couldn't *breathe*, and the pain in her neck didn't stop. She was hot and chilled and freezing and burning and then just numb.

Still, the pain went on and on and on.

24

KULIKA HAD TAKEN a diversion on the way back to the mansion to drop Evita's blood sample off with Dr Ross. She could have taken Evita directly into the lab so the doctor could draw a fresh sample, but Evita had fallen asleep on the drive and frankly Kulika didn't feel like she could spare the blood. They had the sample from Enzo in the cooler, and that was good enough.

Because of the diversion, it was already dark by the time they pulled up at the house, and the evening's festivities were in full swing. There was a foul odour in the air too, something burning and rotten that made Kulika worry about what she had missed in her absence.

Probably best she didn't know. She'd seen enough horrors today to last her a long while.

'There's a room for her in the house,' Monty said, hurrying out of the mansion as Kulika lifted Evita, still sleeping, from the passenger seat. 'The one next to yours.'

'Are you sure?' Kulika asked.

'Captain says,' was all the reply Monty would give.

'Bayly and Enzo are in the back,' Kulika said. 'They won't wake for a day or so, I guess.'

'I'll put them somewhere safe.'

'Where, exactly?'

'Somewhere safe,' was all Monty would say, but Kulika had Evita to look after, so she didn't have much choice but to take the kid at his word. He would only be doing what Bartholomew had ordered him to, and Kulika wasn't in a position to contradict that. All things considered, it seemed best to get Evita set up, then go find Bartholomew herself so she could hear it from the horse's mouth.

In the end, he found her, just as she was leaving Evita's new room.

'Is she well?' Bartholomew said, his voice soft in a way that made it unrecognisable.

'As well as can be expected,' Kulika said, closing the door gently behind her. 'She'll need a lot of blood when she wakes up.'

'She'll get it,' he promised.

'You're very solicitous,' Kulika commented.

That was a mistake. Bartholomew shut down instantly, his usual supercilious demeanour sliding back into place as though it had always been there.

'You've been keeping things from me, Kulika,' he said chidingly, guiding her along the corridor towards her own room. 'About the baron.'

'I'm your Second,' she replied diplomatically. 'You delegate to me. Surely you don't need to know all the details.'

'When they threaten my life and the lives of my crew?' he said, barely controlling the volume of his voice. She'd properly pissed him off now. 'I granted you autonomy when I excused you from drinking at the Convocation,' he said. 'Do you have no appreciation for that? The other Silver in the crew are bound to my blood, but it's been three hundred years since you tasted it. I've given you my trust, and your freedom with that trust. Do we need to revisit that arrangement?'

No.

Every cell in Kulika's body rebelled at the notion. She remembered how it had felt as he'd turned her Silver, forcing his blood down her throat. She remembered the feeding in the breakfast room and how she could taste his spit on the woman's throat.

She absolutely didn't want his blood inside her.

'I'm sorry,' she said, trying to hide her fear. 'It won't happen again.'

'No, it won't,' he said. 'But as luck would have it, I'm in a good mood. Bayly and Enzo are under control, our missing crew members are returned to us, and Cara Alton's body is on its way back to Oklahoma to pose a fascinating conundrum for the local ME's office. By Friday, the stage will be set for our grand introduction to humanity, and we will once again have the freedom we lost three hundred years ago. I'm about to become the king of all creation so, despite the fact that you chose not to inform me that Drake's agent brought a fatal serum into my territory that seems to have transformed a normal failed turning into a handful of unkillable zombies, I've decided to be lenient. Better still, I've left a gift in your rooms,' he added with an indulgent smile. 'Enjoy.' Then he walked away down the corridor whistling to himself, as though he hadn't a care in the world.

Kulika stood blinking for a moment, trying to make sense of Bartholomew's ever-changing moods. Then she heard a disquieting noise from the direction of her rooms, and she was too full of terror to do anything but run.

She flung open the door to find Quick tied to her bed frame by her wrists. Her mouth was gagged, her eyelids fluttering and her skin pale. She was moaning with pain.

'What happened?' Kulika asked, rushing to Quick's side to snap her bonds. They were formed from metal cable, thick and strong, but Quick should still have been able to break out of them, not least by breaking the bed frame.

Which is when Kulika saw the bite on Quick's neck, the bite that wasn't healing.

Bartholomew had drained her.

The *bastard*.

Kulika turned Quick's head so she could untie the fabric gag that cut into the sides of her mouth, then took Quick in her arms and wrapped the blankets from the bed around her body, desperately trying to warm her freezing skin.

'I set the house on fire,' Quick whispered, then she grinned a weak but mischievous grin that set off fireworks in Kulika's chest.

Christ, she was a live one.

But she wouldn't be much longer if Kulika didn't get some blood in her.

Kulika bundled Quick up and laid her gently down on the bed, saying, 'I'll be right back,' then she nipped back next door into Evita's room to fetch the last of the bottles from Bayly's cooler. It took Quick some time to sit up and drink them, with Kulika's help, but when she had, her colour was better, her wounds healed. Kulika could have used the bond to patch her up, but that would have raised questions Kulika would prefer not to answer right now.

It wouldn't be fair on Quick to tell her about the silvering. Not until she was ready.

Maybe never.

'You found Evita,' Quick said, sitting crosslegged in the middle of the bed while Kulika perched on the edge beside her.

'I did.'

'I saw you carrying her. She doesn't look well.'

'She's not. I think she'll get there, though.'

Physically, at least, Kulika thought to herself. Mentally? The woman was strong, but she'd been locked in a box with a monster for months, and Kulika was certain that worse had happened in that lead coffin than Evita had been willing to admit. It would take time to bounce back from that.

'Thank you,' Quick said. 'For bringing her back.' Then Quick reached out and took Kulika's hand in her own, pressing their joined hands together into the soft sheets that covered the bed.

Their eyes locked. It was suddenly impossible for Kulika to ignore that they were in her bedroom together, sitting on her bed, touching each other's skin, palms and fingertips. The room smelled of blood and dirt, but also of dew evaporating in the dawn, frosted autumn leaves crushed underfoot, and bluebell woods bursting with the spring. It amazed Kulika how being close to Quick transported her to another place, how the scent of her skin offered a calm sanctuary as a physical place, far away from South Carolina. Kulika could feel herself reaching for the dream of that escape like a rope in a storm, desperately, in the same way she wished she could reach for Quick now.

'Kulika...' Quick whispered.

Quick reached out to her, then. Her fingertips played tentatively over Kulika's bare shoulder and up the side of her neck until she was holding Kulika's cheek in her hand. It was impossible not to lean into that touch, so Kulika didn't even try to resist. Worse, she reached out to Quick and let herself do the very thing she'd spent the past days dreaming of: she gently brushed Quick's hair away from her face, then sank her fingers into the thick locks up to the knuckle, feeling the weight of them gathered in her palm against Quick's warm neck.

Quick closed her eyes and moaned.

'Kulika,' she whispered again, then she wrapped her hand around the back of Kulika's neck and pulled her closer until they were just a breath away.

Just one taste, Kulika thought.

Then there was a noise. It was a small noise, just a little *click*, like the sound of a latch raising. Kulika wouldn't have noticed had she been even a tiny bit further into the spiral down which Quick's scent was pulling her. But she did notice it, because it was coming from the connecting door that joined her rooms to Bartholomew's.

And Kulika realised she could never touch Quick again. Not like this, not here, where Bartholomew was always watching, listening, *seeing*. The bond between them might be unbreakable except by death, but the new relationship they were building was fragile and precious. Kulika didn't know what it was exactly, because she'd never experienced anything like it before, but she did know it couldn't be like every other short-lived tumble in the dunes that she'd indulged in under Bartholomew's eye.

It had to be different.

But it wouldn't be, would it? For as long as they were here, in this mansion, every moment they had together would be by Bartholomew's gift, at the times of his choosing, by some twisted condition, and within his control. But Kulika could never be anywhere else, either. She couldn't leave the mansion without Bartholomew's permission, not now that Quick was in his power.

She would have killed Bayly today if she'd had to, and Enzo too, just because Bartholomew had asked it of her. He would always be just behind them, watching. There was nothing she could do to stop him.

But she could stop *this*.

'I can't,' she said, pulling away from Quick.

Quick looked surprised for a moment, then hurt, then ashamed, in a rapid kaleidoscope of emotions that Kulika could track as it played out through her scent as well as her expressions. First sharp citrus in the dawn, then peaches bruised at harvest time, and finally those same peaches at the end of the season, forgotten in the leaf litter and made acrid with fermentation.

'We... I...' Kulika pushed herself from the bed. 'I need to check on Evita.'

Quick blinked, schooling her expression, then asked, 'Can I see her?'

Kulika couldn't see the harm. After all, Bartholomew had brought Quick up here, not Kulika. Why shouldn't she see her friend when she was only next door? Besides which, Kulika was feeling guilty enough about what had just happened that she would have done almost anything Quick asked.

Anyway, Bartholomew was watching. If he wanted to object, then let him.

'She's next door,' Kulika said, then she led Quick out of her room and into Evita's.

It was a smaller room than Kulika's, but not by much. This one was arranged as a twin room, with two double beds. It seemed an odd arrangement to Kulika, because it wasn't as though there were any Silver children on the property who might share a room together, but then the crew had grown a lot over the past six months. Maybe they were all sharing rooms now.

Quick rushed to Evita the moment she walked in, falling to her knees at the bedside to take her friend's hand.

'She's cold,' Quick said. 'And thin. And the wrong colour. She's just lying here like— Oh, shit.' Quick turned to Kulika with a look of horror on her face. 'Xiaoyu.'

'What about her?'

'I left her in the woods by the road,' Quick said, panicking now. 'I was trying to get her out of here when I got attacked, and I left her in the woods, but she's ill, Kulika. She's so ill.'

'I'll see what I can do,' Kulika said, turning back to the door. *That* was going to take some explaining to Bartholomew.

'Kulika?' Quick said.

'Yeah?'

'Evita's going to be okay, isn't she?'

Kulika shrugged. 'It'll take time.'

'What happened to her?'

Another thing Kulika had been hoping she wouldn't have to explain.

'She was taken by one of the older members of the crew,' Kulika admitted. 'A friend of mine, I'm afraid. Bayly.'

'Bayly,' Quick murmured, like she was trying to place the name. 'Why?'

'He was going to bargain Evita's life for Enzo's freedom from the covenant. He thought it was the only way to free him. He loves him.'

There was no excusing it, but...

I would have done it for you, Kulika thought.

'So I'm supposed to think that's *romantic*?' Quick said scathingly. 'That's not romantic. That's monstrous.'

'We're all monsters here,' Kulika laughed bitterly. 'Didn't you know?'

But Quick didn't have to be one.

She had the friend she'd come here looking for, and Kulika hoped that would be enough. It would have to be.

She left the two of them alone, and went off to find Xiaoyu.

25

KULIKA HAD ALREADY been sitting at Bartholomew's desk for twenty minutes when he walked into the library at midnight. That had given her time: time to find the old leather-bound covenant book, time to ink the quill, and time to write out a bargain she was ready to sign.

'I've got a new deal for you,' she said as Bartholomew looked at her with interest – and a little disapproval. After all, she was sitting in his chair. She didn't give it up, though. Instead, she turned the open book to face him and drove the quill's nib into her fingertip. 'Read it,' she said. 'I'm ready to sign when you are.'

Bartholomew looked at the book, and at Kulika, then he pulled up a chair on the other side of the desk and sat, pulling the book towards him.

'This is about our Patience, I presume,' he said.

'Yes,' Kulika replied, suppressing the urge to shift anxiously in her seat. She needed him to see that she was serious about this. 'And no. Not *our* Patience. Just Quick, being her own self, out in the world, belonging to neither of us.'

Bartholomew had been reading Kulika's handwritten

bargain, but now he looked up at her in surprise. 'You're giving up your claim on her?'

'If you will too,' Kulika said. 'And your claim on Evita, and one of the humans from the blood cellar. The one I've left in Evita's room.'

He laughed incredulously. 'Just one? Why not all of them? Why not ask me to throw the mansion and the crew into the bargain too? My dear girl, have you lost your mind?' He threw the book back onto the desk, where it landed with a thud that rattled the floorboards. 'If I let them go, what makes you think they won't go telling stories about what we're planning?'

'Does it matter?' Kulika asked. 'You're revealing Cara Alton's body tomorrow. You're revealing us all by the weekend. If anything, the stories they tell are only going to help your cause.'

He considered this for a moment.

'And in return for this generous surrender, what am I getting, exactly?' he asked.

'Me,' Kulika said. 'Forever.'

'Ah,' he smiled, 'but I already have that.'

'Willingly,' she clarified. 'Without argument, as whatever you want me to be. You won't have to bribe me, or blackmail me, or even explain yourself to me. I'll do whatever you want, without question, for the rest of my life, and I'll never try to leave or break that covenant. I swear it, on her life. Whatever you want. Just let her and her friends go.'

'*Whatever* I want?' he asked, his interest sharpening.

'Yes,' Kulika said hopelessly, because she knew there was no other way.

'A blood exchange?'

Kulika gritted her teeth. She'd known it would come down to this, and she knew what it would mean. She'd seen the effect Bartholomew's blood had on his crew. She wouldn't have believed it until the night of the Convocation, but she understood now that there was an extra something in his blood that kept his people close to him. Once they'd drunk enough of it, they didn't want to leave him. Maybe they couldn't.

Kulika didn't want to agree, but she had to. The whole point of this new bargain was to put Quick beyond Bartholomew's influence – and hers – before it was too late. Kulika didn't want Quick to become so bound up in his blood that, like Enzo, she could no longer contemplate being away from him and his crew.

She'd lived that hollow existence herself, several lifetimes ago now, and she wouldn't wish it on Quick for all the free will in the world.

Instead, she surrendered herself to him.

'Even that,' she said.

But still, Bartholomew didn't reach for the book.

'I've offered you everything,' he said. *'Everything.* And am I not delivering? Why give it all up when we're on the brink of victory? You could have everything you've ever wanted *and* our Patience as well.'

'Not like this,' Kulika said. 'Not *our* Patience.'

'Ah,' Bartholomew said quietly, leaning back in his chair. 'I see.'

'Do you?' Kulika asked.

She had to wonder about Evita. It was more than a little surprising that he'd conjured up sufficient feelings to turn her Silver. Back in December, he wouldn't have had the benefit of the BioSilver formula, so he must have had some genuine affection for Evita to make the turn stick. Kulika hadn't realised he had that in him anymore.

Did he feel protective of Evita in the same way that

Kulika was protective of Quick? Was that why he had sent Kulika to find her? And would that make him less willing to surrender her now?

'I understand the instinct to send her away,' Bartholomew said. 'I don't share it, but I understand it.'

'Are you saying you won't give Evita up?'

'No,' he laughed. 'No, I'll happily give her up.'

Kulika was a little surprised by his levity.

'Did you think she actually meant something to me?' he asked incredulously, leaning forward in his chair. 'She's *new*. She's practically still human,' he added derisively. 'Do you really imagine that someone so insignificant could ever mean *anything* to me?'

'Quick means something to me,' Kulika argued. 'She's new.'

'And I won't hold that against you, but really, Kulika.'

'I was new once.'

'And you were fearsome from the very moment you were remade. You didn't forget yourself and become like a true newborn, helpless and pitiful,' he spat disdainfully. 'You remembered it all.'

'And you it hold it against Evita that she didn't?' Kulika asked, trying to understand the expression on his face. On the surface, it was all disgust, but there had been something deeper in his eyes for a brief flash of a moment that made her wonder: did he actually *care*?

Maybe the problem was rather that Evita had remembered everything now, and hated Bartholomew for it. Kulika had told him as much. It had seemed only fair to warn him.

Bartholomew dipped his head, hiding his face. 'Give me the quill,' he said, waving his hand impatiently.

Kulika signed the page quickly before he could change his mind, then pushed the book and quill across the table to

Bartholomew. He pricked his own finger, blending his blood with Kulika's on the nib, and spread the mixture across the paper in his own looping signature. Then it was done, and there was no backing out.

For any of them.

If you enjoyed *A Quick Study*, why not read *Quick and the Dead*? It's the third and final book in the *QuickSilver* trilogy, and it carries on right where *A Quick Study* left off.

***

Join my Readers' Club and receive a FREE short story

www.josiejaffrey.com/subscribe

***

Please leave a review!

If you enjoyed *A Quick Study*, I'd be so grateful if you would please review it. Book reviews can make a huge difference to the success of a novel, particularly those of self-published authors like me. If you have time to leave a review, even if it's just a sentence or two, then I'd really appreciate it.

***

Explore the rest of the Silverse…

This book is just one small part of the Silverse, a whole world of vampires that's waiting for you to explore. There are more novels, short stories, serialised story episodes, and even audio drama podcasts. They're all interrelated, although each series stands alone.

Find out more on my website at www.josiejaffrey.com

Acknowledgements

The QuickSilver series has been a decade in the making. It pulls together threads of story littered over hundreds of years' of world-building, and spread across three other separate novel series and a stack of short stories. Finding those threads and lining them up properly to write this central puzzle piece of the Silverse apocalypse has been an absolute undertaking, and one I would never have been able to manage without the unfailing support of my editor Adie Hart. She goes above and beyond to make sure that I haven't borked the continuity or introduced inconsistencies that will tie me in knots later, and she does so with the kind of enthusiasm that keeps me writing when nothing else would. Thank you so much, A, for everything you do.

Huge thanks also to Jen Sugden, my personal cheerleader and bookseller, and wonderful fellow author. I would not have been able to become an audio fiction writer without your support, and I can't wait to explore the podcast world further with you. Big love.

Thanks also to my author buddies Ali Clack and the UKYA Authors Instagram group for their company and support, and to Rachel Bowdler and the Swords & Sapphics Discord for writing with me. Without the sprints channel in that Discord group, I seriously doubt that this series would have been completed so quickly, and I certainly wouldn't have had as much fun doing it.

And thanks to my street team the Silverse Squad, for their unfailing support in promoting my books. I am so grateful.

Finally – and always – thank you to my husband and son, for everything.

CONTENT WARNINGS

General warning for violence/murder.

General warning for graphic blood/gore, including consensual and non-consensual blood drinking, description of injuries, dead bodies, undead body horror, forensic investigation.

Sexual content (mostly consensual, some dubiously consensual due to coercive control).

Cult-like community with coercive control.

Some swearing (up to and including 'fuck').

Emotionally abusive/coercive relationships, including family.

Memories of child neglect and abuse.

Uncomfortably sexual behaviour from a quasi-father figure.

Dubiously consensual voyeurism.

Graphic description of being burned, once by sun and once by arson.

Description of immortal characters buried alive.

Discussion of historical piratical crimes.

Mentions of slavery, both in real/historical context and fantastical/modern context, including keeping humans imprisoned for use as a blood bank.

Mentions of cannibalism.